921176-0

W9-CZV-381

DATE DUE

MAR 1 1			

Body Image

Other Books of Related Interest

Teen Decisions Series
Dating
Dieting
Drugs
Sex

Opposing Viewpoints Series
America's Youth
Eating Disorders
The Family
Health and Fitness
Mass Media
Sports and Athletes

Current Controversies Series
Teen Addiction

Contemporary Issues Companions
Depression
Eating Disorders
Teen Addiction
Teens and Sex

At Issue Series
Anorexia
Bulimia

Body Image

Auriana Ojeda, *Book Editor*

Daniel Leone, *President*
Bonnie Szumski, *Publisher*
Scott Barbour, *Managing Editor*
Helen Cothran, *Series Editor*

GREENHAVEN
PRESS ®

San Diego • Detroit • New York • San Francisco • Cleveland
New Haven, Conn. • Waterville, Maine • London • Munich

LIBRARY OF CONGRESS CATALOGING-IN-PUBLICATION DATA

Body image / Auriana Ojeda, book editor.
   p. cm. — (Teen decisions)
   Includes bibliographical references and index.
   ISBN 0-7377-1256-2 (lib. bdg. : alk. paper) —
   ISBN 0-7377-1255-4 (pbk. : alk. paper)
   1. Body image in adolescence. [1. Body image.] I. Ojeda, Auriana, 1977– .
II. Series.
   BF724.3.B55 B63 2003
   306.4'61—dc21
                                                     2002066462

Contents

Chapter 3: Body Modification and Cosmetic Surgery

Chapter 4: How to Improve Your Body Image

Foreword

The teen years are a time of transition from childhood to adult-hood. By age 13, most teenagers have started the process of physical growth and sexual maturation that enables them to pro-duce children of their own. In the United States and other indus-trialized nations, teens who have entered or completed puberty are still children in the eyes of the law. They remain the respon-sibility of their parents or guardians and are not expected to make major decisions themselves. In most of the United States, eigh-teen is the age of legal adulthood. However, in some states, the age of majority is nineteen, and some legal restrictions on adult activities, such as drinking alcohol, extend until age twenty-one.

This prolonged period between the onset of puberty and the achieving of legal adulthood is not just a matter of hormonal and physical change, but a learning process as well. Teens must learn to cope with influences outside the immediate family. For many teens, friends or peer groups become the basis for many of their opinions and actions. In addition, teens are influenced by TV shows, advertising, and music.

The Teen Decisions series aims at helping teens make re-sponsible choices. Each book provides readers with thought-provoking advice and information from a variety of perspec-tives. Most of the articles in these anthologies were originally written for, and in many cases by, teens. Some of the essays fo-cus on ethical and moral dilemmas, while others present perti-nent legal and scientific information. Many of the articles tell personal stories about decisions teens have made and how their lives were affected.

One special feature of this series is the "Points of Contention," in which specially paired articles present directly opposing views on controversial topics. Additional features in each book include a listing of organizations to contact for more information, as well as a bibliography to aid readers interested in more information. The Teen Decisions series strives to include both trustworthy information and multiple opinions on topics important to teens, while respecting the role teens play in making their own choices.

Introduction

Body image is defined by health professional Carla Rice as "an individual's experience of his/her body. It is the mental picture a person has of his/her body as well as the individual's associated thoughts, feelings, judgments, sensations, awareness and behavior." Thus, body image is not just how one looks, but how one feels and acts in response to their perceived appearance. Body image changes over time. As Rice states, "Body image is not a static concept. It is developed through interactions with people and the social world, changing across life span in response to changing feedback from the environment."

Body image is especially important during the teen years. Teens' bodies change from childish lines to feminine curves and masculine angles. At the same time that these physical changes are occurring, teens are becoming intensely self-conscious. Due to the combination of rapid, dramatic physical development and growing self-awareness, teens are particularly attuned to the image their bodies project—and they are particularly susceptible to reaching distorted conclusions about their bodies or taking drastic measures to repair perceived bodily defects.

A Growing Concern

Statistics reveal an alarming preoccupation with body image in adolescents and children. Recent studies have found that the number one wish of girls between the ages of eleven and seventeen is to be thinner, and girls as young as five years old have voiced concerns about gaining weight. According to the Council on Size and Weight Discrimination, young girls are more afraid of becoming fat than they are of nuclear war, cancer, or losing their parents. Over 90 percent of high school junior and senior women diet regularly, even though only 10 to 15 percent are considered overweight according to standard height-weight charts.

This preoccupation with weight and body image puts many teens at risk for developing an eating disorder. According to the Eating Disorders Association, "Eating disorders develop as outward signs of inner emotional or psychological distress or problems. They become the way that people cope with difficulties in their life. Eating, or not eating, is used to help block out painful feelings. Without appropriate help and treatment, eating problems may persist throughout life." Eating disorders include anorexia nervosa (self-induced starvation), bulimia nervosa (binge eating followed by purging), and binge or compulsive eating (consuming large quantities of food in a short period of time). People with borderline eating disorders exhibit risky eating habits and an unhealthy preoccupation with food, but to a lesser extent than people with full-blown eating disorders. Anorexics and bulimics adopt dangerous practices to control their weight, such as smoking or taking drugs to control their appetites, vomiting or taking laxatives to purge their bodies, and over-exercising. Over long periods of time, eating disorders can result in irregular or loss of menstruation, skin problems, irregular heartbeats, kidney and liver damage, loss of bone mass, hair loss, infertility, cardiac arrest, and death.

Teenage boys are also affected by body image concerns, although they primarily strive to build muscle mass and gain weight. Some boys struggle with weight loss issues, especially if they are teased for being overweight or if they participate in weight-restrictive sports, such as wrestling or gymnastics. Experts estimate that over 1 million boys and men struggle with eating disorders and borderline conditions. Many boys try to sculpt their bodies to fit a "buff" ideal, and some go to dangerous lengths to achieve this look. Some boys take anabolic steroids—synthetic compounds that mimic the action of the male sex hormone testosterone—to increase their muscle mass and improve their athletic performance. If taken in excess, anabolic steroids can cause impotence, shrunken testicles, breast enlargement, damage to the heart, kidneys, and liver, and halted bone growth. These practices are particularly risky during adolescence because of the dramatic physical changes that take place during puberty.

The Process of Puberty

Puberty is a period of biological maturation that includes all the changes that take place when children become adults. Puberty begins when hormones—chemical substances produced by an organ, gland, or special cells that are carried in the bloodstream to regulate the activity of certain organs—prepare the body for reproduction. Puberty typically begins between the ages of eight and thirteen for girls and nine and fourteen for boys and lasts about three to four years.

The first sign of puberty in girls is breast development, which occurs at an average age of about ten and a half. Breast development is followed by a growth spurt, the growth of pubic and underarm hair, and an increase in oil and sweat production. A girl's first period, or menarche (occurring at an average age of twelve and a half to thirteen), follows an increase in the growth of pubic hair and the external genitalia and occurs about two years after puberty begins. Around this time, a girl's body increases its stores of muscle and fat, but the ratio of muscle to fat changes from primarily muscle to equal amounts of muscle and fat. She reaches her final adult height about two years after menarche.

Puberty generally begins later in boys, at an average age of eleven and a half to twelve. Boys first notice an increase in the size of their testicles, followed later by the growth of pubic and underarm hair and penis size. They then undergo a growth spurt, deepening of the voice, an increase in muscle mass, the ability to get erections and ejaculate, and the production of more oil and sweat. At this time, some boys develop breast tissue, called gynecomastia. This is followed by the development of chest and facial hair. Boys experience their peak growth spurt about two to three years later than girls.

The Effects of Puberty

All of these changes can negatively affect a teenager's body image. Often hands and feet grow faster than other parts of the body, which can leave teens feeling gangly and awkward. Increased oil and sweat production can cause acne problems. Teenagers are developing intellectually at the same time that they are developing physically, and body image can be greatly affected by these transformations. Hormones that cause physical development also cause changes in mood that affect how a teenager perceives his or her body. To complicate matters, teenagers develop at rates that differ according to their genetic makeup. Seeing bodies that are more or less developed than one's own can lead to feelings of isolation and doubt about whether one is normal or attractive.

It is common for a young girl's self-esteem to plummet in early adolescence. Her body image is often negatively affected by her sudden accumulation of fat, especially on her breasts, hips, thighs, and buttocks. Even though she is developing womanly curves that are necessary to later house a baby, many girls become concerned about their weight. They become preoccupied with the "ideal" body size and shape and generally associate perfection with thinness. Girls who mature early are at the highest risk for poor body image and developing an eating disorder because many compare their curvy bodies to their peers' thin, childish bodies and think that they are overweight. These girls are more likely to develop risky eating and exercise practices such as "crash" dieting (drastically cutting caloric intake in a short period of time), smoking, and overexercising. These habits can lead to dangerous eating disorders like anorexia and bulimia.

According to the Harvard Eating Disorders Center, "Most dissatisfied girls want to be thinner, while about equal numbers of dissatisfied boys want to be heavier. Boys want to grow into their bodies, whereas girls are more worried about their bodies growing." When guys go through puberty, they may feel skinny or awkward, and they may feel gangly because of hands and feet that are too large. Boys who develop gynecomastia suffer poor body image over the growth of breast tissue, and they may avoid swimming or changing clothes in front of their friends out of embarrassment. Gynecomastia may disappear with normal development and exercise, but if it does not, cosmetic surgery may be an option. Most boys focus on becoming more muscular and strong as they strive to replicate society's ideal body.

Media Images

Teenagers learn what society considers an ideal physique primarily from the media. They are bombarded with images in magazines, movies, on television, and in music that decree what is fashionable and attractive. Recent studies have found that by the time a woman is seventeen years old, she has received over 250,000 commercial messages through the media. Girls see images of teen girls and women who are unrealistically thin. Experts claim that fashion models weigh 23 percent less than the average female; an average model is five feet eleven inches tall and weighs 110 pounds, while an average woman is five feet four inches tall and weighs 140 pounds. A young woman between the ages of eighteen and thirty-four years has a 7 percent chance of being as thin as a catwalk model and a 1 percent chance of being as thin as a supermodel. Models and many actresses are abnormally thin, but teenage girls who are not thin may view these images and believe that something is wrong with them. One study found that 47 percent of the girls interviewed were influenced by magazine pictures to want to lose weight, but only 29 percent of the girls were overweight. Experts conclude that viewing images of extremely thin celebrities may negatively influence teenagers' body image.

Boys' body images may be negatively influenced by media images of smooth, perfectly sculpted torsos. According to advice columnist Mike Hardcastle, boys have recently been introduced to the concept of the "perfect male form." He contends that for decades men were measured in terms of career success, power, and financial security, but the feminist revolution in the 1960s, which demanded equal rights in the home, workplace, and education for women, changed that. Hardcastle states that "as women started to build killer careers of their own, males started to feel the pressure to attract women with 'rugged good looks,' 'buff bods,' and 'chiseled features.' Today, boys feel the same pressures to be physically attractive as girls do, even if this pressure manifests in different forms." For boys, the perfect body is tough and strong, but for girls the perfect body is slim and toned.

Some experts argue that toys such as G.I. Joe and Barbie may influence children's body image. Both dolls are unrealistically proportioned; if the 1999 G.I. Joe were a real man, he would have a massive fifty-five-inch chest and bulging twenty-seven-inch biceps. An average real-life man who is about the same height as G.I. Joe and fairly athletic has biceps that are about eleven and a half inches around. Similarly, a life-sized Barbie doll would measure a thirty-eight-inch bust, eighteen-inch waist, and thirty-four-inch hips. The average woman measures a thirty-seven-inch bust, a twenty-nine-inch waist, and forty-inch hips. Some critics contend that this unrealistic ideal of physical flawlessness may make children insecure with their own looks and lead to poor body image and eating disorders later in life.

Cultural Shifts in Body Ideals

The prevailing ideal body images reflect the values of the culture. Currently, America's ideal body images reflect values of youth, health, and wealth. The popular ideal body is toned, tanned, and lacks excess fat. This image projects youthfulness, healthy food choices, self-discipline, exercise, and sufficient wealth to enjoy leisure time in the sun. This ideal body represents values that are important to today's society. Other cultures and time periods have valued different body types for different reasons.

In the 1950s, the ideal of female beauty was epitomized by actresses Marilyn Monroe and Jane Russell. They were exaggeratedly feminine, with soft, fleshy bodies, curvy hips, and large breasts. The 1950s are commonly known as the "baby boom era" because there were so many marriages made and babies born when the survivors of World War II came home. The war heroes brought back ideals of feminine beauty that emphasized voluptuous, "womanly" bodies. They represented the nurturing and fertile aspects of womanhood that were so prized during the post–World War II era.

The sexual revolution in the 1960s changed the ideal female form, and boyish, skinny figures were in fashion. A waifish young model named Twiggy, who was five feet six inches tall and weighed only eighty-nine pounds, was heralded as the ideal. As feminists left their homes and entered the workplace, they demanded equal treatment from their employers and their husbands. The beauty ideal shifted to accommodate women's growing independence; she no longer reflected nurturing motherhood, but disregard for conventional femininity.

Although male body ideals have received less attention than female bodies, they also have changed with cultural seasons. In the 1950s, society valued a gruff, masculine ideal, similar to John Wayne. He represented a physically intimidating man who would provide well for his family. Today's ideal man is slender, but with broad shoulders, well-defined legs and stomach, and strong arms. He represents a nurturing man who is less threatening than the man of the 1950s. Today's society values men who are physically strong, but who also share in household duties and child raising.

Forming Your Own Body Image

Knowing that today's ideal body is another passing trend does not lessen the desire teenagers have to adhere to the current ideal and be attractive. However, it is important to remember that the current standard of extreme thinness for women is unrealistic and impossible for most women to achieve. The sculpted body of most male models is difficult to achieve without the aid of anabolic steroids. Rather than striving for the ideal, try to keep your body healthy by exercising regularly and eating nutritious foods. Five servings of fruits and vegetables every day can increase your energy, improve your health, and reduce your risk for certain types of cancer and heart disease. Regular aerobic exercise can increase your energy, strengthen your cardiovascular system, and improve your immune system. Feeling healthy can boost your self-esteem and your body image.

The selections in this volume, many written by teenagers or people recounting their teen experiences, are aimed to enrich your understanding of what body image is and how to improve yours. The articles in Chapter One, Common Concerns About Body Image, provide factual articles and personal accounts on eating disorders, obesity, and other body image questions. Chapter Two, Body Image and the Media, includes information on the connection between images of beauty in the media and body image issues. Chapter Three, Body Modification and Cosmetic Surgery, discusses the dangers and rewards of voluntarily altering your body. The articles in Chapter Four, How to Improve Your Body Image, provides information on nutrition, exercise, and building your self-esteem. *Teen Decisions: Body Image* is meant to help you put current beauty standards in perspective and improve your body image and self-esteem.

Chapter 1

Common Concerns About Body Image

Confronting an Eating Disorder

Sara Eisen

In the following article, Sara Eisen argues that many young people damage their bodies in their quest for physical perfection. She claims that some teenagers starve themselves (anorexia) or binge and purge (bulimia) in an attempt to achieve the perfect figure. Others may overeat as punishment for their flaws or lack of willpower. Eisen contends that even many teenagers who are not anorectics or bulimics have unhealthy eating habits that may lead to more dangerous practices. She suggests that if you or someone you know shows signs of an eating disorder, seek professional help immediately. Eisen is the director of the Teen Center for WholeFamily.com, an Internet community that offers advice to parents and teenagers to build strong relationships.

I magine your parents gave you a car for your 16th birthday. It's not new or anything, but it doesn't have too many miles on it. It's an OK color, not your favorite, but OK. It's got two or three nicks or scratches, but it's pretty cool, and it moves like crazy.

Now imagine that you looked at that car, the one that takes you to school every morning, the one that takes you to the mall every weekend, the one that feels so good on the highway, with the windows rolled down, imagine that you looked at that car and saw every bump and every scratch and the wrong color and the wrong upholstery and you hated it.

You hated that it was not a Porsche, not a BMW, not a Ferrari. You hated it so much, that you decided to punish it. Decided to let it know who was boss. You hated it so much that it was making you hate everything else, too. It was all you could think about. So you stop changing the oil. You stop filling it up. You just let it run down, that stupid, hateful, undeserving, ugly hunk of tin.

Body Breakdown

This seems ridiculous, right? But every day, millions of young people across America are starving their bodies, letting them break down, because they are not pretty enough, not thin enough, not Jennifer Aniston, not Heather Locklear, not Calista Flockhart. Not "perfect." They hate themselves, hate their bodies, hate their lives. How much sense does this make? Not much. But to a sufferer of an eating disorder, it is very, very real.

There are no easy answers as to why someone decides to let their body starve, or eats the entire refrigerator and then makes themselves throw up, or abuses laxatives. No easy answers why some people exercise for three or four hours a day to burn off two cookies, or why some people just can't stop eating because they hate themselves so much they think they deserve to be fat and unhealthy.

Impossibly Thin

Many people attribute eating disorders to society: Hollywood and the media demand an impossible standard of thinness, and young people feel that in order to be attractive, they need to look like Jennifer Love Hewitt. They feel that their entire self-worth is tied up in their appearance, in looking tiny. And that if they can't, they are worthless. This may be part of it.

But there are other issues, too. Many people use eating disorders as a way to control something in their lives. They figure that a battle with food is one they can win.

Others want to be the "most" something—so they decide to

Eating Disorders Have Become Common

Anorexia nervosa. Bulimia nervosa. These medical terms have become common lingo because millions of adolescent girls and women struggle with these diseases. "The number of people with eating disorders and borderline conditions is triple the number of people living with AIDS," says Carolyn Costin, director of the Monte Nido Residential Treatment Center. And the number of people with undiagnosed eating disorders just keeps getting higher. Considering the fact that 80 percent of American women are dissatisfied with their weight, the Eating Disorders Awareness and Prevention Organization estimates that thousands, if not millions more people than the 10 million statistic are actually suffering from a food disorder but think that they're just dieting normally.

The scary reality is that girls who have an eating disorder usually keep it secret for years before receiving treatment—willingly or forcibly. These girls either hide their problem, or don't realize that they have a problem at all, which is termed a "borderline" eating disorder. And no one knows exactly how many girls have borderline disorders. They obsess over calories, occasionally turn to laxatives or vomiting to lose weight, and exercise incessantly after overeating but still manage to avoid raising suspicious eyebrows from family and friends. When left untreated, borderline conditions can spiral into serious and devastating disorders, even death.

Cylin Busby, *Teen Magazine,* May 2001.

be the "most" thin. It is an obsession, like any other, only more dangerous.

Some people have a need, for whatever reason, to be perfect—and equate this with being perfectly thin.

Others are seeking to be "invisible"—literally; they strive to be lighter than air.

> Every day, millions of young people across America are starving their bodies, letting them break down.

Some people use starving as a form of rebellion against their parents. Food is just another power struggle with Mom or Dad.

Others are trying to draw all the attention to themselves in an attempt to get their parents to stop fighting, to try to keep them together.

Many people hate themselves so much, they are punishing themselves. They feel that they do not deserve the pleasure derived from eating.

And others are practicing a form of passive suicide. Many of them succeed.

Kicking Out Body Image Demons

The debate among experts on the causes and ways of curing eating disorders—anorexia, bulimia, and compulsive eating are the main ones—has been going on for a long time. The theories change regularly, against a backdrop of people clamoring for more attention to be paid to this crucial area of illness. They are right; eating disorders and their casualties will not go away by themselves. More often, they take on a life of their own, becoming an actual "voice" in a person's head. The voice is comfy there; it will stay unless it is vigorously kicked the hell out.

I suggest you read up on the subject, if it interests you, or if you think you may be suffering from an eating disorder. . . .

But whatever you do, do not tell yourself that you are "on a diet" or "living healthy" if you have just radically dropped loads of weight in a short time, or if you exercise more than you know you should. Do not tell yourself that you "are just having a midnight snack" if you regularly consume a whole pint of ice cream when everyone is sleeping.

You are fooling yourself. Or worse, you know exactly what you are doing, but you are lying to everyone else. That voice inside your head is not only making you nuts, it's also making you dishonest.

So get help. Tell someone—a parent, trusted adult, guidance counselor, older sibling. You can not beat this alone, but you must beat it. Before it beats you.

Body Dysmorphic Disorder

Nutricise.com

Body dysmorphic disorder (BDD), a condition in which people become obsessed with a perceived physical defect, is a growing problem among young people. Many people think their noses are too large or their lips are too thin, but people with BDD allow their concern for certain body parts to affect their schoolwork, social lives, or family relationships. In the following article from Nutricise.com, the author explains how BDD can seriously disrupt a teenager's life and suggests that those who suffer from BDD seek professional help. Nutricise.com is a comprehensive online resource for nutrition and fitness information.

How you look, or rather, how you *think* you look, can affect the way you feel about yourself. There's probably a reasonable connection between the two for most people. For example, you may not feel so confident about doing an oral presentation if you feel that you're having a bad hair day, or maybe you get bummed out when you've got a couple of blemishes. On the flip side, if you find yourself constantly being concerned that everyone is gawking at your hair because it's unflattering in some way, or if you're worried people's attention is focused on your less-than-perfect complexion or your weight that you cancel school-related activities and dates with friends, you're in dangerous psychological territory.

Imagined Ugliness

Body dysmorphic disorder (BDD), often called imagined ugliness, is a preoccupation with a defect in one's appearance (weight, complexion, hair, face and legs are the most common fixations)—often an imperfection that exists only in the person's mind. As many as 5 million people in the United States may have BDD, and while the disorder strikes both men and women of any age, adolescence may be the most common time of onset—news that may not be all that surprising considering that high school is often the first time in a person's life when attractiveness equals popularity and acceptance.

In an environment in which it seems like you have to be Britney Spears's twin to get a prom date, how much stressing over your looks is normal and how much constitutes a real psychological problem? "There's no clear division," explains James Rosen, professor of psychology at the University of Vermont, "but you begin to have a problem when you attach more importance to your appearance than is realistic. If you think that if you don't look perfect nobody could ever care about you, or you think that people are repulsed by you, that's not normal. Looks *do* make a difference, at least initially. To a degree we all judge a book by its cover so to speak, but when people

> As many as 5 million people in the United States may have BDD.

come to choosing their friends, it's usually based on a personality and a sense of values."

The symptoms of BDD can range from mild to very severe. In its most extreme cases, BDD can "completely destroy lives," says Katharine Phillips, M.D., author of *The Broken Mirror:*

Understanding and Treating Body Dysmorphic Disorder. She tells of one extreme situation involving a young woman who'd been diagnosed with BDD during high school and had grown increasingly worse over the years. She lived with her parents and hardly ever left her bedroom; when she did, she covered her face with a veil.

> You begin to have a problem when you attach more importance to your appearance than is realistic.

Certainly not every case of BDD is so severe: Some teens even may function so well that their families don't recognize that anything is wrong, says Phillips. "They may be turning invitations down and pulling out of social circles a little bit."

A Vicious Cycle

To someone with a healthy self-image, though, even the mildest symptoms are shocking. For example, in a recent study by Phillips and other doctors specializing in the disorder, many participants spent all their time worrying about the defects they felt they had. They could think of nothing else. The disorder creates a vicious cycle. Most people with BDD tend to withdraw from social activities, but withdrawing from others because you think they won't accept you usually only worsens the problem. For example, if you won't talk to guys because you feel as if they're staring at your body and wondering why it's not more like Christina Aguilera's, you may inadvertently start sending out the vibe that you're unfriendly—which will make guys stay away from you, which will confirm your fears that you don't measure up and that therefore you're undesirable.

So what should someone with BDD do? For many, facing their fears is the way to go, says Rosen. "It's a little like overcoming a phobia of driving after being in a car accident," he says. "You're not going to get over that fear until you get behind the wheel again."

Some sufferers of BDD are beyond the point of helping themselves. Several studies have suggested that antidepressant or anti-anxiety drugs are effective for many patients with severe symptoms. Often people think that cosmetic surgery is the answer; most of the time, however, it's not, because the problem is actually in your mind. "I usually advise against it," says Phillips. "Surgery is irreversible, and most people with BDD usually feel like it didn't work anyway."

If you think you may have BDD, you should talk with a friend or a mental health practitioner about it. If you think a friend may be suffering—for example, she won't play sports or go to the beach because she believes her legs are too bulky—confront her. It may be difficult, but ultimately it could help. Left untreated, BDD usually only gets worse.

The Problem of Obesity

Eileen H. Shinn and Carlos Poston

In the following article, Eileen H. Shinn and Carlos Poston contend that the percentage of people suffering from obesity has increased steadily in the past forty years. Some people argue that obesity is the result of genetics, but Shinn and Poston maintain that obesity is often a result of poor eating habits and lack of exercise. They suggest that the best way to maintain a healthy weight is to eat more fruits and vegetables, eat smaller portions than are often served in restaurants, and exercise regularly. Shinn is a postdoctoral fellow at the Center for Health Promotions and Research Development at the University of Texas Health Science Center's School of Public Health. Poston is an assistant professor in the Department of Medicine and Behavioral Medicine Research Center at Baylor College of Medicine in Texas.

A s people struggle to keep their resolutions to lose weight and maintain a healthier diet, they might appreciate the fact that they are not alone in these efforts. As classified by the most current standards, 55 percent of men and women in the U.S. are estimated to be overweight or obese, and these prevalence rates have steadily increased over the last forty years. Data from the Framingham study, one of the most well-known and well-respected long-term studies conducted in the United States, show that child and adolescent obesity rates have increased as well in the last 35 years.

Defining Obesity

In 1998, the National Institutes of Health defined obesity as a body mass index of 30 or above. [Body mass index can be calculated by dividing your weight in kilograms by height in meters, squared—or—by dividing your weight in pounds by your height in inches, squared, and then multiplying that number by 704.5.] One's risk for developing associated diseases or dying of obesity-related conditions increases considerably at this cutoff. There is a lesser, but still considerable, risk for disease and death associated with being overweight, which is defined as having a body mass index of 25 to 29.9.

It is a common perception that being obese or overweight is the result of a person's genetic makeup. However, Dr. Claude Bouchard, a well-known obesity geneticist, has stated that genes play only a modest role in the problem of obesity in the U.S. Although the body of research linking specific genes to susceptibility for obesity has uncovered intriguing results, these findings tend to be very complex and difficult to apply to the current epidemic of obesity in the U.S. Furthermore, no research has established the existence of genes necessary for the development of obesity (i.e., genes that, if present, will clearly cause obesity).

Many experts instead believe that the high rate of overweight and obese Americans is due to environmental factors. Dr. Boyd Eaton and his colleagues hypothesize that the problem of obesity in America is a natural result of the mismatch between the modern lifestyle of convenience, versus the lifestyle for which humans evolved.

> 55 percent of men and women in the U.S. are estimated to be overweight or obese.

In other words, while modern technological advances have provided us with labor-saving devices and abundant food supplies, our bodies are still adapted to more primitive times when food was in shorter supply and physical activity demands were greater. For example, it is estimated that in the Paleolithic era, the typical human diet had 10% to 20% of its calories from fat, compared to the current American diet of about 32% of calories from fat. Indeed, we have increased our average total caloric intake by almost 200 calories in the last decade alone. Further anthropological studies of hunter-gatherer societies suggest that humans were significantly more active, compared to our current activity levels in western societies. Therefore, strong evidence exists that the two main factors that are responsible for the upswing in obese and overweight people in America and other industrialized nations are overconsumption of food and physical inactivity. Let us further explore some of the contributing factors behind these trends.

> The high rate of overweight and obese Americans is due to environmental factors.

Overconsumption

One of the reasons that we eat too much is that portion sizes in both cookbooks and restaurants are several times larger than the recommended standard serving amounts. For example, while the standard serving for meat is 3 ounces (e.g., the size of a deck of cards), restaurant portions typically start at 7 to 8 ounces and climb up to 22 to 38 ounces. A medium-size movie theater popcorn consists of 16 cups (the standard serving is 3 cups) and some soda servings can be as big as 44 ounces (the standard serving is 12 ounces). These "super-sized" portions contribute to our increasing overall caloric intake, and counteract the efforts we may be making to specifically reduce the fat in our diets.

It is human nature to underestimate our food intake. Several recent studies used new methods (referred to as "biochemical validation") to accurately determine each person's daily food intake (as opposed to the old method of self-report). These studies found that most people underreported their total caloric intake. Furthermore, obese individuals were even more prone to these reporting errors, sometimes by as much as 47%.

Overconsumption also results from the erroneous belief that it is acceptable to eat more calories, as long as one follows a " low-fat" diet. One study showed that people who were told that they had just eaten a low-fat lunch went ahead and ate more calories later in the day, compared to when they were told they had eaten a high-fat lunch. Therefore, the idea that we are lowering our fat intake may encourage us to eat more calories.

Inactivity

Less than 10% of American adults engage in regular and vigorous physical activity, and nearly 60% report having a sedentary lifestyle. The amount of time spent watching television is a major determinant of sedentary lifestyles, and appears to have drained our will and capacity for physical activity. For example, the prevalence of obesity is over 4 times greater among individuals who watch 21 or more hours of television per week, compared to individuals who watch less than 7 hours per week. In children, the amount of time spent

> Portion sizes in both cookbooks and restaurants are several times larger than the recommended standard serving amounts.

watching television is one of the strongest predictors for obesity. Studies have shown a direct relationship between hours of television watched and the development of obesity in children.

Next Steps

Based on the contributing factors discussed above that lead to weight gain, what can we do? Everyone who has heard the saying "eat a balanced diet and engage in regular exercise" knows that it is easier said than done. However, there are some steps you can take to promote a healthier environment in your home.

1. Throw away all junk food and make a concerted effort to limit your access to other types of high-calorie/ high-fat snacks or fast food. Replace these foods with fresh fruits or vegetables instead.

Less than 10 percent of American adults engage in regular and vigorous physical activity.

2. Keep a record of the foods you have eaten during the day and get a sense of the size of your typical portions. This will allow you to recognize harmful patterns and make adjustments accordingly.

3. Incorporate physical activity into your daily routine. You may want to start small, such as taking the stairs at work or parking your car further away from entrances. Once you begin to make these small steps, we recommend using five behavioral principles to start a regular exercise regimen:

• Keep a log of your exercise. This important step will increase your awareness of the amount of physical activity that you are getting each day.

• Cue yourself to exercise, and remove barriers to exercise. Lay out your exercise clothes and shoes the night before, and set your alarm a half-hour earlier. Set up an exercise time with a friend.

• Reward yourself for exercising and meeting your goals. Treat yourself to a new magazine, book, or CD (do not use food as a reward).

• Manage your stress, because high stress is a predictor of exercise avoidance behaviors. Remind yourself that exercising is an excellent stress-reduction technique.

• Finally, start thinking about exercise as a necessary way to make yourself healthier and more resistant to chronic diseases, rather than seeing it as a chore.

Weight related health issues are a serious concern in the U.S.

Although genes may certainly play a contributory role, much of the problem can be attributed to environmental causes. Regardless of our genetic makeup, we tend to eat too much and to not exercise enough. However, there are several things we can do to counteract these tendencies. Instead of focusing on fat intake, Americans should cut portion sizes, since there is good evidence that reducing total calorie intake is the most important factor in weight loss. Increasing physical activity is the other necessary step, and can be more easily incorporated into daily routines using the behavioral techniques mentioned above.

So if you come from a family in which being overweight is very common, don't despair. Being overweight is not preordained by your genetic code and losing weight is within your control. By arming yourself with both information and good techniques, you are well on your way to making significant lifestyle improvements.

My Sister Had Anorexia

Jason Dean

In the following article, broker Jason Dean describes his sister Allison's bout with anorexia. According to Dean, Allison evolved from a healthy teenage girl to an eighty-three-pound stranger who needed to be hospitalized. Dean contends that his sister's anorexia caused tension within the entire family. With the help of counseling, Allison recovered from her anorexia, and Dean and his family learned to cope with her struggle to control her eating disorder.

In the 12th grade I received an A on an assignment I wrote on anorexia nervosa. Four years later, when my sister was in 12th grade, she lived with anorexia. So did our whole family.

Starting Out Small

Allison started dieting when she was in junior high. She often tried new diets. At the time, her behavior seemed normal enough to me. Many girls in their teens count calories and diet.

But soon it became clear that Allison was developing an abnormal attitude about her weight and her body. She began dieting so much that the tension around the kitchen table at meal times grew. Most days she ate two plain bagels; one for breakfast and one for lunch. Due to our busy schedules, I was never really sure if she ate dinner at all. I tried to convince her that she

didn't need to diet and that she looked better before she started becoming so obsessed about her weight. But as she began distrusting her own view of her body, mine meant nothing.

Allison couldn't fool the people in her life. "Her body used to be so toned, now she's all bones. Her skin looks so dry and pale. I swear she's shrinking. What's wrong with your sister?" were just some of the comments people made.

At her lowest point, Allison weighed 83 pounds. It was clear to all of us that Allison needed to be hospitalized.

Going Inside

I'll never forget the day our mom took me to visit her at Toronto's North York General Hospital. Visions of the way she looked still haunt me. I especially remember how awkward her head looked on her fragile neck as she looked around at us; forcing a smile for her visitors. Her nurses wouldn't let her shower that night—fearing that she might faint in her weakened condition.

Still, weeks passed before Allison admitted having a problem. My mom encouraged me to visit Allison on my own. I was up for anything that would help my sister, but a solo visit terrified me. I was still analyzing why Allison was anorexic. What would I say to a sister I barely recognized?

When I walked into Allison's hospital room, I was surprised to see Allison beginning to look like her old self again. We started up with the usual patient/visitor chitchat and then the room became silent. I started thinking of our shared memories as brother and sister. Most memorable were the thousands of times Allison, a talented artist, unveiled her latest paintings. While I was lost in thought, Allison broke the silence. "They're stuffing so much food in me; I feel like jumping out the window!"

> Allison was developing an abnormal attitude about her weight and her body.

I didn't realize at the time that her comment might have been therapeutic for her. Instead, hearing her allude to suicide made me feel useless. I was supposed to be there to make Allison feel better!

When it was time for me to leave, Allison, sensing my reluctance to go, walked me to the elevator and said, "I love you" as the elevator doors closed. I smiled, because those three words also seemed to be saying, "I understand how hard this must be for you. Seeing you was support enough."

Beginning to Heal

Shortly after my solo visit, all of us began to participate in family counseling sessions. I expected the family counseling sessions to revolve around Allison, but we got into topics that we rarely discussed at home.

The social worker explained that when a family member is struggling with a problem, the problem can be like a pebble that is thrown in a pond—"The pond represents the entire family. The ripples represent the family's problems. The pebble triggers ripples that cover the entire pond the way a family crisis spreads throughout an entire family."

The ripples of Allison's anorexia had touched our whole family, even the family cat had a change in behavior during the time that Allison was away at the hospital.

Soon after the final family counseling session, Allison weighed in at 110 pounds and her nine-week hospital stay ended.

I remember back before Allison's struggle with anorexia, she saw me doodling a woman leaning against a sports car. She laughed and said, "Sometimes our drawings show what we're deprived of and our deepest desires!"

In her paintings, my sister Allison creates beautiful worlds of birds, butterflies and lakes filled with still waters. I know some people battle anorexia for a lifetime, but I feel that Allison and my family are one step closer to reaching calm waters.

I Had Bulimia

Sandy Fertman

In the following essay, an anonymous teenage girl describes her experience with bulimia to the author, Sandy Fertman. She describes enormous food binges that she and her twin sister indulged in and later regurgitated. She and her sister thought that they kept their bulimia secret from their friends and family; she later found out that other people knew about the problem but did not know how to confront her. Her friends staged an intervention, which prompted her to seek medical help. She contends that the support she received from her friends and family helped her recover from her bulimia. Sandy Fertman is a contributor to *Teen Magazine*.

I guess I'd say I had a pretty normal childhood.
I grew up in a house in California with my older brother, Jackson, and my identical twin sister, Carey. My sister and I have always been really close, but it's hard not to be when you're identical twins. My father is a psychologist and my mom owns a travel agency, but they were separated when I was about five. Carey, Jackson and I lived with our mom. Still, my dad has always been very much a part of my life.

My mom has always been overweight. I think her fears of us

getting fat were instilled in us, even though she never voiced them. I first became aware of my own weight when I was around fifteen years old. One day, I looked in the mirror and noticed my face was changing. It looked kind of heavy and I thought, "Oh, my God! I have to lose weight!" It just hit me like a punch in the stomach.

From age seven, I had been a gymnast. I wasn't thin, but I always had to be aware of my body. But by the time I was fifteen, I was also modeling and acting, so I really had to start watching my weight.

The Family Secret

I had this diet of eating only steamed vegetables. One night, I ate too many vegetables and felt really sick. My mom said, "Oh, Kelly, just throw up." I said, "No way! That's so disgusting!" Mom said, calmly, "Just do it, Kelly. You'll feel better." She told me to just stick my finger down my throat. So I did and after that, it became a habit, a really long, bad habit.

I felt a sense of power after that first time I purged. I thought I felt great that first night.

Both my sister and I learned how to purge that way. Carey and I would even throw up at the same time! We didn't think there was anything wrong with it. My mom knew the first couple of times, but then we decided we'd keep it our secret.

> If we ate a lot at any meal, we'd both have to sneak out and "get rid of it."

That secret lasted five years. I thought I'd kept it a secret from my friends, but later I found out they all knew. Your friends always know. They see how much you eat and you think you're being sneaky, saying you exercise a lot or that you have a fast metabolism. But after you come out of the bathroom and your face is all puffy, your eyes watery and your nose runny, they know what's going on. They just didn't have a clue what to do about it.

Living a Lie

My sister and I didn't really talk about our purging, but we both understood that if we ate a lot at any meal, we'd both have to sneak out and "get rid of it." After dinner at home, I'd usually run a bath to disguise the noise of vomiting. If I couldn't find a bathroom, I'd drive somewhere and get rid of it—in a bathroom, the bushes, wherever. At parties, I'd just "get sick" in the bathroom after eating a lot of snacks. I usually could do it faster than someone could go to the bathroom! I'd eat until I was uncomfortable and then just go get rid of it. . . .

I hardly ever ate fatty foods, because I was still watching my weight, but a few times a week I'd say, "Well, I can eat anything I want!" so I'd eat a donut or two and then purge. I got a lot of attention from being thin and at the time, that made it all worth it to me. In fact, most bulimic girls are never obese; they're usually average in weight, but want to have that "edge" over other girls. I felt inferior to everyone else, so I'd think, "If I can only have control over this one thing, I'll be able to make up for all my deficiencies."

I Felt Unworthy

Obviously, I didn't have much of a sense of self-worth and truly didn't like myself a lot, never thinking I was smart enough, pretty enough or funny enough. You feel like you're not worthy of being loved or even liked. So you get into this self-destructive behavior, thinking that if you're thin, it will compensate for all your inadequacies. But even though you think you've got it under control, you're way out of control!

> The worst feeling was that I felt like a fraud all the time.

The worst feeling was that I felt like a fraud all the time, always keeping this secret, hiding this habit. I was so ashamed. It's such a secret that your whole life becomes centered around keeping it. I chose friends that could never get close to me, because if they did, they'd figure out my little secret. In my case, though, I was lucky to still have my childhood friends, but the people I really began to hang out with were very emotionally detached and distant people. That's what I wanted.

> I simply lost interest in school and everything about it.

During the whole time I was eating and purging, I never had a boyfriend. I didn't feel lovable; I figured no one would want me. I dated a lot, but even to this day, I haven't gotten serious with anyone. I was very social, but it was always very superficial, like going to dances and hanging out with large groups of friends, nothing intimate. It was really easy to hide my problem from the guys I dated, because no one assumes you're going to the bathroom to vomit. . . .

I was always faking it, always full of lies and excuses to enable me to keep my secret. I'd say to my friends, "Oh, I've gotta get going" or "I've gotta run some errands," nonspecific excuses so I could go munch out and throw up. Your life revolves around eating. It got to a point where I didn't need to use my finger or anything. My muscles just did it. . . .

Eating Me Up Inside

I was always an A student, but during my senior year, I got kicked out of high school. I simply lost interest in school and everything about it. I was just so bored and I had started hanging out with this group of friends outside of school who I called the low-lifes. I just didn't care about anything anymore, except my habit, of course.

Things went from bad to worse that year. By then, I was throwing up six times a day, every day. One afternoon, I was sitting in traffic school and I suddenly got this tingling feeling in my hands and then my muscles started contracting and curling up and contorting. My whole body just froze! I excused myself and went to the pay phone to get help and when I started walking back, I screamed, "Oh, my God!" and I collapsed on the floor by the classroom—my legs were paralyzed. I couldn't move any of my muscles, even my tongue! My mom came to get me and said we'd wait until the morning to see how I felt. I said, "Mom, I may not be alive in the morning!" so she drove straight to the emergency room.

The doctor examining me told us I had had a minor heart attack. He explained that I had hardly any electrolytes left in my body from throwing up so much. Those minerals maintain your heart and muscle activity, basically everything. My mom, of course, had known I was bulimic, but now she, too, had to face up to it. The nurses immediately injected my vein with a needle and hooked me up to this potassium drip. It was the worst pain I have ever felt in my life, like razor blades going through every vein in my body! You can feel it going into your arms, your shoulders, your heart, your stomach, your thighs, your legs and your feet. It's like someone is taking razor blades soaked in salt and alcohol and dragging them slowly through your body. I was crying through the whole procedure, "Please stop it! Please, please!" But it was either that or I'd die. . . .

> I really believed that [getting fat] was worse than having a heart attack!

I stayed overnight in the hospital and you'd think I would have learned my lesson, but I didn't. I started throwing up right afterward. I felt like the alternative to purging was getting fat, and I really believed that was worse than having a heart attack!

Everyone told me I had to see a therapist, so I went to a counseling group at the local university medical center for a short time.

Friends to the Rescue

My true friends decided it was time to take action, so they did an "intervention." That's when your friends and family get together and confront you all at once with your problem. My sister and four friends showed up at my house and all day long they kept saying, "Kelly, you're so smart and so beautiful, you don't need to do this!" They said they just didn't understand how I could do this to myself, basically letting me know how much it was hurting them. I felt like I was really disappointing them, like something was really abnormal about me. That's what really made me feel like I had to do something about my bulimia; I felt so incredibly ashamed.

> Battling bulimia was the bravest thing I've ever done.

The intervention was actually wonderful because my secret was finally lifted off of my shoulders. As painful as it was to be told I was, in a way, a failure, it was good for me. I realized I needed help. . . .

After that intervention, I stopped purging. By that time, Carey was already going to group and individual counseling and was taking medication to treat her bulimia. I never did any of that. But only a year later, I started throwing up again. I hadn't broken the habit. I ended up having another minor heart attack while I was driving home from the gym one day. Even at the hospital while I was getting that horrible potassium drip, I was wondering, "How can I keep eating and getting rid of it without dying?" I can't believe that I was that out of control!

Just one week later, I was back in the hospital with another heart attack and that's when I thought, "Oh, my God! I can't control this!" That's when I decided to stop it for good.

Filling Myself Up

It's been three years now and I feel great. Although I've never gone to therapy, I do talk to another recovering bulimic about it. I knew I didn't want to die and I started realizing who I was and that I really did like myself.

I took the proficiency test to graduate from high school and then went on to graduate from the local university magna cum laude. Now I have my own television production company and I'm producing an outdoor-related TV series. I really love my work. Actually, most bulimics are very ambitious people.

They're into that "control thing" so they know what they want and are inspired to go to extremes to get it—not that that's always good.

My whole life has changed without the pressure of hiding a secret and supporting a habit. All of a sudden, you have an empty part of your life you have to fill. It's like when you end a relationship with a boyfriend: You've been seeing him and then all of a sudden he's not there anymore. That's what I'm doing now. Battling bulimia was the bravest thing I've ever done. Now I have to face those fears of "getting big" and having no one like me. Today, I'm fifteen pounds heavier than I was when I was bulimic, but I think I'm in good shape. And most importantly, I'm really happy.

Boys and Eating Disorders

Stephanie Booth

In the following article, *Teen Magazine* contributor Stephanie Booth presents a teenage girl's experience with her bulimic boyfriend. Although eating disorders are more common among girls, an increasing number of boys, especially athletes, demonstrate symptoms of anorexia, bulimia, or overeating. Many sports, such as wrestling or bodybuilding, require males to monitor their weight and food intake. Sometimes boys, like the narrator's boyfriend, take these restrictions to extremes, and they threaten their health with harmful eating and exercise habits. If you notice similar patterns of behavior among your friends, notify someone who can help them fashion healthier eating habits.

If you really are what you eat, most of my girlfriends would be grapefruit, fat-free yogurt and diet cola. If my now ex-boyfriend Josh was what he ate while we were dating, he'd be a glass of water and one leaf of lettuce. Or maybe a handful of vitamins and some granola. Or when he was in a binge phase, just a huge pile of junk food.

You probably think food obsessions are strictly a girl thing. I

used to believe it was only females who freaked out about dieting, exercising, trying to be "good" and then giving in and pig-
ging out. Then I hooked up with Josh.

His Perfect Body

An awesome athlete, Josh was very much aware of his body and
what he put into it. When I first met him, he was eating bee
pollen cakes to increase his stamina for rock climbing. "I know
it's weird," he shrugged, unwrapping one at the movies after
buying me buttered popcorn and peanut butter cups. Then, all
during the movie, he kept whispering: "How's that popcorn?
Good? And the candy? It sure looks good." I thought he just
wanted to make sure I was having fun.

All that summer, Josh would come to the pool where I was a
lifeguard and swim for about two hours straight every day. He
had a perfect build—broad shoulders, washboard stomach, muscular arms and legs from lacrosse and running. He also read
every health and fitness magazine on the market. "Guess what I
just found out?" he'd say when he'd greet me after his swim. Before even kissing me, he'd launch into a lecture about how a certain mineral was supposed to burn fat or something.

One night when we were on the way to a party, he told me
about the juice fast he was on. "Can you believe it?" he said. "I
haven't eaten since Wednesday."

"You must be hungry," I answered. It
wasn't until we passed a Taco Bell that it
finally hit me. "Josh! It's Saturday!"

How can I describe his face? He
looked relieved, guilty, pleased, proud.

> Josh was very much
> aware of his body
> and what he put
> into it.

"I know," he said. "Man, I'm starving. I nearly passed out after
swimming today."

I made him pull into the next fast-food place. Josh didn't pro-
test. He ordered two hamburgers, a fish sandwich, a large choco-
late shake and two orders of fries. We sat in the parking lot and

he inhaled everything. I was so proud of myself for "taking care of him," I didn't realize how unhealthy it was.

On the way to the party, we stopped three more times. Once, so Josh could get some frozen yogurt,

> I was so proud of myself for "taking care of him."

and again so he could pick up a box of granola, "to balance out the junk food," he explained. The third time, Josh just pulled over to the side of the road and threw up. He said it was just because he hadn't eaten in so long, and then ate too much too fast. So when I saw him chowing on potato chips and brownies at the party, I figured he was on empty again and needed to refuel.

His Messed-Up Mind

As summer progressed, Josh and I became inseparable. I trusted him and never believed he would cheat on me. Only thing was, I was beginning to feel a little jealous of food. If we were watching TV and a pizza commercial came on, Josh would be glued to the screen. At the mall, he'd walk by the food court four times, reading each menu as though there would be a test later. For days, he'd only eat lettuce and vinegar, then devour a large pepperoni pizza and two foot-long subs in one sitting.

After a while I had to confront the fact that Josh's habits were beyond weird. The evidence was mounting. First I found glycerin suppositories in his backpack (OK, I was snooping), then laxative gel caps in his locker at the pool.

"Guys don't get eating disorders!" my best friend laughed when I confessed my suspicions. She told me I was being paranoid, so I tried to ignore his behavior. But it was hard. Especially one time when he ate dinner at my house. My mom had made her famous pot roast, and at first Josh just pushed it around his plate. But Mom wouldn't let up on him, so after he finally finished everything, she stood over him and asked: "How about seconds?" Josh jumped up and ran to the bathroom. When he came back, he heaped his plate high, scarfed and went to the bathroom again. I excused myself and quietly walked up to the bathroom door. I could hear him throwing up.

It wasn't until my birthday that I snapped. Josh arrived holding an enormous bouquet of yellow roses. "I'm here to sweep you off your feet," he grinned, and pulled out two tickets to the concert I'd been dying to see. When we went outside, though, Josh's car wasn't in the driveway.

Similar Factors for Boys and Girls

The characteristics of males with eating disorders are similar to those seen in females with eating disorders. These factors include low self-esteem, the need to be accepted, an inability to cope with emotional pressures, and family and relationship problems. Homosexuality and bisexuality also appear to be risk factors for males, especially for those who develop bulimia. Homosexuality can be seen as a risk factor that puts males in a subculture that places the same premium on appearance for men as the larger culture places for women. Both males and females with eating disorders are likely to experience depression, substance abuse, anxiety disorders, and personality disorders.

Office on Women's Health, "Boys and Eating Disorders," *Eating Disorders Information Sheet*, 2000.

"I thought we'd walk," he said, smiling. "It's not that far."

The theater was clear across town, almost ten miles away! "You've got to be kidding," I said.

"I want to walk!" Josh exploded. "You're so lazy!"

"I never realized how psycho you are!" I shot back. As awful as it sounds, I felt relieved saying it aloud.

I wish I could say those words had a magic effect on Josh, too—that he'd suddenly realize he had a problem—but that's not what happened. Josh broke up with me then and there. I ran to my bedroom and cried.

Boys and Bulimia

Two days later, Josh passed out in history class. His parents told the emergency room doctor what they knew of Josh's odd eating and exercise habits; the doctor got suspicious and called in a psychiatrist. That's how Josh got diagnosed as having an eating disorder.

Although it's easier to recognize in women, more than 1 million men—especially athletes—in the United States suffer from an eating disorder. There's no exact cause, but almost all sufferers are perfectionists and overachievers. Controlling what they eat gives them a sense of being in control of their lives, when in reality, the food is really controlling them.

> After a while I had to confront the fact that Josh's habits were beyond weird.

Josh didn't just have bulimia (bingeing and purging) or anorexia (where you refuse to eat at all or exercise nonstop); he had symptoms of both, what doctors call an "atypical eating disorder." As soon as he was released from the hospital, his parents admitted him into an eating disorders program. He was lucky to have found a great therapist, and a program that had guys like him in it—one was a triathlete Josh had read about in a magazine.

Josh has his eating disorder under control now, but he's not "cured" and is still in therapy. We never did get back together, but we're now good friends. Even with him away at college, we e-mail each other a lot. "Some days I still feel like if I don't puke right now, I'm going to explode," he told me recently. "Other days it's not so bad. But I still can't imagine eating whatever I want, just because I'm hungry."

I hope one day he can.

Chapter 2

Body Image and the Media

The Media Focus Too Much on Looks

Diana Vancura

In the following viewpoint, Diana Vancura argues that the media emphasize appearance over talent, which negatively affects the body image of teenagers. She maintains that television and magazines advertise a specific body type as beautiful, which ignores the many forms beauty can take. She suggests that society should try to focus on people's accomplishments rather than their looks. Vancura is a contributor to Teen Advice Center, an online community of teenagers and young adults who share problems and give advice.

What is up with the portrayal of women in the media today? If you turn on your TV right now and look through the channels most of the women you'll see will be twig-like and made over with loads of makeup. Flip through a magazine, and you'll be greeted by a bunch of airbrushed models positioned in poses that hide their "flaw." Even at your school, can you find one girl that doesn't have makeup on? Why are young women today encouraged to be something they aren't? Why aren't we encouraging women to be themselves and to feel comfortable with their own, unique beauty, instead of throwing images of anorexic, computer-generated beauty queens in their faces?

From "Beauty Brainwash," by Diana Vancura, www.teenadviceonline.org, October 18, 2000. Copyright © 2000 by Teen Advice Center. Reprinted with permission.

Models Aren't Real

It's practically impossible to have a good body image these days. It's hard enough comparing yourself to the prettiest girls at your school, but it's completely impossible to compare to the women in magazines and on TV! You want to know why? They just aren't real. Like anybody in real life has a makeup artist reapplying their makeup every few minutes and a personal stylist to find clothes that complement their bodies. Then if we try to stop making TV a bunch of perfect

> Flip through a magazine, and you'll be greeted by a bunch of airbrushed models.

clones, nobody cooperates. When a well-known actress with beautiful curly hair cut off her long locks for a less flattering hair style, the ratings of her show decreased. Now, this girl is a very talented actress who works on a very well written show, but when it comes down to it, what matters is . . . her hair? Is this crazy or what? When new shows pick their stars for their acting abilities and not their looks, read the reviews. Very seldom will you read about how well they play the character. Instead you read about how so-and-so is too pudgy to star in a series.

There's been a trend of young stars posing in provocative magazines. These young women are all talented actresses/ singers/whatever, but why do they feel the only way they can be accepted is if people marvel at the way they look half dressed and airbrushed? What about the little girls that look up to these stars? What kind of message are they sending them? Even our own families are concentrating too much on our looks. After a play I was in, one girl in a leading role greeted her parents after a wonderful performance. What was the first thing they said to her? "Honey you looked so beautiful!" Forget about all the talent it took for her to make her character come alive. Forget the courage it took for her to get up in front of dozens of people from our school and community. The first thing her parents thought to compliment her on was the way she looked.

Many Forms of Beautiful

I'm also not saying appreciating our looks is a bad thing. Our bodies are beautiful and we should appreciate it, but we also shouldn't try to make ourselves all look "perfect" or obsess over our looks. There are lots of ways to be beautiful and I think its sad that the media seems to be telling us we need to have the "look" of the moment or we simply aren't good-looking enough.

I'm not saying I'm not guilty. I often find myself complimenting my sister on how pretty she is, instead of her artistic ability or amazing wit. I also spend lots of time in the mirror criticizing my flaws or trying to hide them with makeup. I am a hypocrite, but if I promise to try to compliment my friends and families on their accomplishments instead of their looks and to focus on what's inside instead of what people look like, will you promise to do the same? Maybe together, we really will start to make a difference.

Media Images Are Unrealistic

Hilary Rowland

In the following article, Hilary Rowland argues that the media present unrealistic images of beauty. Actresses and models are significantly thinner than other women, she contends, and the images in magazines are strategically altered to make the model look perfect. Rowland maintains that these images cause everyday people to feel insecure about their own bodies, even if they have nothing to feel insecure about. Rowland is a contributor to *Fazeteen.com*, a Canada-based online periodical that provides teens with thought-provoking articles on current issues. In addition the author is involved with two similar websites: www.hilarymagazine.com and www.newfaces.com.

I t's bikini season again and this year the trend to be thin is more pronounced than ever.

The newsstands are displaying magazines of which almost every issue has a thin, gorgeous swimsuit model on its cover. Your television is showing more and more unhealthily thin actresses. Bones are jutting out and implants are taking the place of real breasts. Most of these supermodels and actresses are so unnaturally thin that they risk infertility, osteoporosis and, ultimately, kidney damage.

Jennifer Aniston's former trainer says "[Jennifer's] new figure did not come from working out with me. She lost body fat (seemingly all of it) by drastically reducing carbs in her diet—a way that's not healthy in my books."

Obsession with Thinness

This obsession with thinness seems to be a sort of domino effect. One actress loses weight to please the media, next all her co-stars are losing weight to keep up. Courtney Thorne-Smith (size 4) has said that if she were not on the TV show *Ally McBeal,* she'd be 5 pounds heavier but won't risk it for fear she'll look big next to her size 2 co-stars. "I would run eight miles, go to lunch and order my salad dressing on the side. I was always tired and hungry," says Courtney.

> Your television is showing more and more unhealthily thin actresses.

Meanwhile, her co-star, Calista Flockhart, has discovered spinning—vigorous workouts on stationary bikes. "At first it hurts your butt, but you become addicted to it like a maniac," says the size 2, 5'6", 100 pound *Ally McBeal* star.

Does anyone ever think about how the overload of these images in the media affects the everyday person? Well, for many women, and an increasing number of men, it doesn't exactly have a positive effect. In fact, the idea of the media's (and consequently, everybody else's) "ideal" woman often makes "normal" people self-conscious—even if they have nothing to be self-conscious about.

Media Images Are Touched Up

What most people don't realize is that every image of a model or actress in a fashion or beauty magazine has been touched up using the latest computer technology to remove "flaws" like bulges, pimples and stretch marks. Elizabeth Hurley even admitted that her breasts were electronically enlarged for the cover of *Cosmopolitan* magazine.

"On my last Cosmo cover," she recalled in a recent *Details* mag interview, "they added about five inches to my breasts. It's very funny. I have, like, massive knockers. Huge. Absolutely massive."

Christy Turlington explains to *Elle* magazine . . ."Advertising is so manipulative," she says. "There's not one picture in magazines today that's not airbrushed.". . .

A Thin Ideal

Advertisements emphasize thinness as a standard for female beauty, and the bodies idealized in the media are frequently atypical of normal, healthy women. In fact, today's fashion models weigh 23% less than the average female, and a young woman between the ages of 18 and 34 has a 7% chance of being as slim as a catwalk model and a 1% chance of being as thin as a supermodel. However, 69% of girls in one study said that magazine models influence their idea of the perfect body shape, and the pervasive acceptance of this unrealistic body type creates an impractical standard for the majority of women.

Mediascope Issue Brief, "Body Image and Advertising," April 25, 2000.

"It's funny," Turlington continues, "when women see pictures of models in fashion magazines and say, 'I can never look like that,' what they don't realize is that no one can look that good without the help of a computer."

Beyond that, there are about 100 to 300 professional photographs taken for each published image you see. They are taken from the absolute best angle in perfect lighting with the clothes pinned just so.

And as if that wasn't enough, the models' hair and makeup is always professionally done and is constantly touched up by a makeup artist and hair stylist standing by to make sure nothing looks less-than-perfect.

Unhealthy Weight

According to *Prevention* magazine, a "healthy weight" for a woman who is 5'9" is 129 to 169 pounds. An average 5'9" model's weight is somewhere around 115 pounds.

Cindy Crawford is an example of an exception to the rule: She is a model and she is not stick-thin. She has lots of muscle, and it looks good. She is the kind of woman more magazines need to have on their covers and in their editorials. She projects strength and beauty.

"I am not the skinniest model," says Cindy, "but I have had success as a model, so I feel more confident putting on a bathing suit and standing in front of a camera. In life, I have all the insecurities anyone has. It's a cliché, but we're our own worst critics."

Male Body Stereotypes

Chris Godsey

According to Chris Godsey, emphasis on male physical beauty in the media may contribute to negative body image in boys and young men. He contends that repeated images of perfectly sculpted, hairless male torsos influenced his own self-esteem and maybe the self-esteem of other young men. Although Godsey claims that he is fit and active, he still compares his own physique to celebrities' bodies and unsuccessfully strives for their perfection. He argues that less emphasis should be put on looks because focusing on appearance leads to self-doubt and insecurity. Godsey is a contributor to Adiosbarbie.com, a website dedicated to celebrating different body types and rejecting impossible beauty standards.

B rad Pitt is a beautiful man. I'm a male, I'm straight, and I don't mind admitting that Brad's body, especially in the movie "Fight Club," is an impressive sight. Same with rapper D'Angelo, in that powerful, sexual "Untitled" video; he's a put-together dude, and there's no reason to deny it.

But while I'm cool with thinking those guys are fine, I'm bothered by my occasional inability to see them, *Men's Health* magazine, or any Soloflex commercial, without honestly believ-

Excerpted from "How Does It Feel?" by Chris Godsey, www.Adiosbarbie.com, 2000. Copyright © 2000 by Adiosbarbie.com. Reprinted with permission.

ing that unless I have three percent body fat, a hairless torso and washboard abs, I'm a sorry human being.

I spent the week after watching "Fight Club" counting calories like Sarah Ferguson; if I catch "Untitled" on *MTV Jams* before heading to work in the morning, I usually skip breakfast and double that day's workout.

> I've realized my motivations are more superficial than healthy.

After a long time believing I run, lift, bike, hike and try to "eat right" in the interest of being fit, I've realized my motivations are more superficial than healthy. Instead of seeking true mental and physical fitness, I worry about appearances—about what I'm convinced I should look like, based on magazines, movies and MTV.

I go through streaks of avoiding certain foods not because they taste bad or otherwise disagree with me, but because I'll feel guilty after eating them . . . like getting freaky with Little Debbie or Sara Lee is something I should be ashamed of.

Healthy, but Discontent

The thing is, I'm actually in pretty decent shape—about 6'2", 200 pounds, and relatively solid. I don't lift much, but I do a lot of pushups, pullups and crunches, and I run and bike about 80 miles a week. Most of the time, I usually eat whatever I want, and while I'm working some back fat and a little extra around the middle, I'm not doing too bad. I'm not ripped, but I'm not flabby, and I'm healthy enough to feel lucky.

Still, since high school, I haven't been content. On an intellectual level, I understand that every human body is different, and that there are no "right" and "wrong" ways to look, and that I don't have to live up to anyone's standards but my own.

But what are my standards? A few years ago, I lived with a bodybuilder who was my height, plus 40 pounds, and about four percent body fat. I felt skinny and soft and sub-par that whole year. Now, I live with a competitive runner who weighs about

140, and if I'm not careful, I start feeling like an oaf, all big and clumsy and excessive.

My head just about explodes trying to find a balance between what women want to see, what constitutes fitness, and how much (and why) I actually care. It's tough to observe my own standards when they never stay the same, and when they're manipulated by forces I don't always comprehend.

Why Am I Discontent?

So what the hell is going on? Why do I spend so much time in the mirror, flexing and twisting and prodding and scrutinizing every part of my body that I deem less than perfect? Why can a Polo Sport ad inspire me to denounce all fat and commit every waking moment to some sort of muscle-building or cardiovascular activity? Why, after my girlfriend tells and shows me in 50 different ways that she considers my physical presence a religious experience, do I ask her if she's attracted to me? It's like I'm a . . .

I don't want to say it, but it's true. It's like I'm a woman. My sense of self-esteem too often depends on how I see my body, and my body image is increasingly affected (infected?) by a continuous, arbitrary onslaught of images and messages that dictate the rights and wrongs of physical appearance. And I'm not the only guy going through it.

I've got buddies who are manly men—who would punch me for saying what I did about Brad Pitt—but who get real touchy about what their asses look like in a pair of jeans. I know dudes who won't eat anything that's not low-fat, non-fat or otherwise tasteless because they "need to lose a couple pounds." Just the existence of magazines like *FLEX* and *Men's Fitness* proves that men provide a viable market for folks looking to make money by exploiting bullshit ideas of perfection.

> It's tough to observe my own standards when they never stay the same.

I used to wonder why every woman in *Glamour* and *Shape* is impossibly gorgeous and half-dressed—I couldn't figure out why women (straight women, at least) wanted to gawk at sexy pictures of other women. Then I realized something: They don't want to see those models, they want to be them.

Boy Toys

Some analysts say boys are increasingly bombarded with the sorts of cultural messages that many say have contributed to eating disorders in young girls. A study by doctors at McLean Hospital in Belmont, Mass., published in July 1998, found that "boys'" toys, such as G.I. Joe action figures, had grown more muscular over the past 20 years. The researchers said that trend was likely to make boys feel more ashamed of their bodies, and become obsessed with lifting weights to bulk up. "Haven't we learned anything from the research done on female eating disorders . . . except to extend it across the gender line?" asks Kevin Coleary, a doctoral student in education at Harvard University. "You would think we would have learned to make our culture more accepting of healthy, natural physiques," he writes in the *New York Times* (June 22, 1999).

Issues and Controversies On File, April 14, 2000.

Somebody way smarter than me figured that out a long time ago and started making serious cash selling women images and ideas that breed dissatisfaction and self-doubt.

Men are also consumers, and we're just as receptive to the suggestive sell. Now, somebody's making money off our insecurity, too. Karma's for real, baby, and it's coming to get us.

Conflicting Messages

This is complicated stuff, man. Why do so many people obsess about body image? Do we want to look good for other people, or for ourselves? Are we trying to attract a mate, or prove our dominance over the competition?

Do conflicting messages breed insecurity and self-abuse? Or are magazines and movies just mirroring a culture that values style over substance, looking good over feeling good, and what sells over what's right?

One thing I do know: Body image is no longer an exclusively female problem. In fact, men now have 10% of all eating disorders. Body image isn't limited by race, culture, religion, social or financial status, education or geography either. It's a human problem, and it runs remarkably deep. And since we caused it, I'd like to believe we have the ability to fix it.

Where do we start?

Countering the Dieting Myths

Sarah Schenker

In the following article, nutrition scientist Sarah Schenker contends that obesity is a serious public health problem that is increasing across the world. At the same time, people are more body conscious than ever, and the struggle to reduce waistlines and eliminate cellulite often leads people to adopt unhealthy weight loss and exercise habits. Popular dieting myths, such as low-carbohydrate or high-protein diets, offer quick weight loss results, but Schenker claims that the results are short-lived and may be harmful to your body. Schenker maintains that a healthy, balanced diet that includes lots of fresh fruit and vegetables and regular exercise is the best way to reach your body's ideal weight and maintain your health.

Fad diets are everywhere. If you believe what various celebrities and women's magazines are preaching, high-protein diets, detox diets, food-combining diets and such like are the saviours of the Western world—here to save us from becoming fat. Perhaps you have been tempted to try one yourself or know of friends, relatives, or patients who are on them. We do

From "The Truth About Fad Diets," by Sarah Schenker, *Student BMJ,* September 2001. Copyright © 2001 by the British Medical Association. Reprinted with permission.

need all the help we can get as obesity rates are climbing like never before. But what happened to good old-fashioned healthy eating? Too boring and not trendy enough? We asked Sarah Schenker, a nutrition scientist at the British Nutrition Foundation, to shed some light on the subject.

Obesity can lead to premature death and cause considerable ill health and is one of the largest and fastest growing public health problems across the world. In England, 17% of men and 21% of women are obese, and over half the population is overweight. However, there seems to be more importance given to body image than ever before. For this reason many people, obese or not, are spending a considerable proportion of their income on information or treatments that claim to help tackle their "weight problem."

For the past 20 years the consensus of nutritional advice has been to eat less fat and more complex carbohydrates and fresh fruit and vegetables. But such an approach is often considered too simple, too boring, or too slow, and desperate people will often take desperate measures. Many of the books, products, and clinics available exploit the slimmer's desperation and obsession with weight, shape, and appearance by feeding them a succession of half truths and bogus science, claiming to assist in their attempts to lose weight. By buying into these fad diets many obese and overweight people have tried but failed to lose weight or maintain their weight loss but have spent a small fortune. Despite this, the enthusiasm for quick fix diets seems to be undiminished. Also, in such a climate opposing views on dietary strategies will always attract attention. Given the prominence of many of these alternative solutions, it is hardly surprising that the public is frequently confused by the apparent mixed messages.

Diet Myths

The most popular dieting myths currently around are:
- The "detox your system" diets will not just cause weight

loss but will banish cellulite and cleanse the body.

• Particular foods or combinations of foods such as those found in cabbage soup can boost metabolism and speed up weight loss.

• Poor digestion of foods or "allergy" to foods can cause weight gain.

• Protein-containing foods and carbohydrate-containing foods should not be eaten at the same meal.

• It is carbohydrates that are fattening and should be eliminated from the diet.

• Your blood group or any other physiological characteristics can dictate which foods you should and should not eat.

Diet Myth Number 1

Many celebrities are detoxing their systems through diets that exclude wheat, dairy products, sugar, caffeine, and alcohol. This regimen will apparently cleanse your blood, flush out toxins, and so aid weight loss, and is claimed to be particularly effective in getting rid of cellulite. Cellulite is not a unique type of fat that requires special treatment and it is not caused by toxins. It is just a build up of fat in areas where people are predisposed to lay down fat. For women this tends to be the hips, thighs, and bottom, and nothing can change your genetic makeup. Regular exercise and healthy, balanced eating will eventually lead to weight loss but a few "wobbly bits" may still remain. Exercises targeted at specific muscle groups in problem areas are the best remedy.

> Obesity can lead to premature death and cause considerable ill health.

Diet Myth Number 2

Soup diets promise a miraculous instant weight loss of up to ten pounds in the first week and attribute this result to the special combination of ingredients. Very often when people start to diet they find that they can lose a relatively large amount of weight in the first week. Then the weight loss slows down and they start to feel demoralized and often this is when they give up, only to repeat the cycle a few weeks later. There is no magic, rapid way that fat stored in our bodies can be lost. During the first week of a diet, especially an extreme diet such as fasting or very restrictive diets that eliminate most foods, people usually lose carbohydrate stored as glycogen, and the water that has been absorbed with it. We have approximately 500 grams of stored glycogen (that will last a sedentary person about three to four days) and each gram is stored with 3 grams of water resulting in 2 kilograms weight loss. Once this is lost, and if it is not replaced, fat loss will dominate, but being much more energy dense than carbohydrate, it requires a greater calorie deficit to be used up. There is no healthy way to lose weight fast.

> [Cellulite] is just a build up of fat in areas where people are predisposed to lay down fat.

There are no special combinations of foods that will affect the metabolism one way or the other. Overweight people do not usually have slow metabolisms, in fact quite the opposite. The bigger a person is, the harder the body has to work, for instance to pump blood around the body and carry the large frame when they move, so the higher the metabolism and the energy requirement. This means that a very large person can easily lose weight on 1500–1800 calories a day if they are only burning up 2500 calories. As they become lighter their calorie requirement will drop but this can be compensated by increasing the exercise level and lowering intake to maintain the deficit.

Diet Myth Number 3

People suffering from food allergies or food intolerances do not gain weight by eating the culprit foods, in fact quite the reverse, as food intolerances often cause sickness and diarrhoea or both.

Food allergies can have very serious consequences resulting in anaphylactic shock [a total body allergic reaction]; milder reactions include asthma and eczema. None of these are pleasant but they are not responsible for weight gain.

Diet Myth Number 4

Dr. William Hay invented "food combining" at the beginning of the last century. He believed that disease resulted from the accumulation of toxins and acid waste in our bodies. The way to cure disease was to avoid eating "foods that fight." In his opinion, you should not mix proteins and carbohydrates in the same meal, and you should eat foods which restore the body's natural balance between acids and alkalis. To date there is no scientific evidence to support this theory. The rules of food combining are rather complicated to observe and inherently contradictory, and the whole idea of food combining is nutritional nonsense. It is possible to lose weight observing the regimen but this is because it greatly increases the intake of fruit and vegetables at the expense of more calorific foods and also considerably restricts the types of food eaten (which may make it more difficult to meet nutritional needs). So while it is not harmful, people should not be fooled into thinking that food combining per se offers any nutritional benefit.

> There is no magic, rapid way that fat stored in our bodies can be lost.

Diet Myth Number 5

In the high protein, low carbohydrate diet you are encouraged to eat all the meat, fish, eggs, and cheese you want, but have to cut out potatoes, bread, pasta, and fruit. Even the slimmer's favourite energy snack, the banana, is banned. The theory goes that it is sugar and not fat in the diet that makes a person fat. Sugar is rapidly absorbed into the blood stream causing blood glucose levels to increase.

Insulin is then required to bring levels back to normal. Insulin also happens to be the hormone responsible for promoting fat deposition.

Up to here this theory is correct but irrelevant to dieters. By taking in fewer calories than are being used up, fat stores will be used as a source of energy. Not only do low carbohydrate diets go against all current healthy eating advice but they can lead to ketosis. This causes the pH of the blood to fall which can lead to unconsciousness and eventually coma. Anyone trying to exercise while following this diet will find it a real problem as stored carbohydrates are the best source of energy for exercise. This diet is likely to make the person feel tired, lethargic and irritable.

> There are no special combinations of foods that will affect the metabolism.

Diet Myth Number 6

Diets based on the idea that a person's physiological characteristics, such as eye colour, hair type, or blood group, can dictate which foods are likely to cause weight gain have no scientific basis. The idea behind blood group diets is to split foods into groups of "highly beneficial," "neutral," and "avoid," depending on type.

For instance, people with blood group O are told to avoid sweet corn as this will cause weight gain, whereas it is acceptable for those with a different blood type; people with blood group A are told kidney beans will encourage weight gain. Both sweet corn and kidney beans are low in fat and high in fibre so it is difficult to understand why this should be the case. A person may well lose weight on this diet because it is so restrictive, but in being so is also likely to make the diet unbalanced. Daily consumption of fruit and vegetables of all types should be encouraged to help prevent diseases such as heart disease and cancer.

Blaming obesity on genes, metabolism, or mysterious outside

forces does not help individuals to face up to the control they have over their own body weight. Acknowledging the contribution of personal lifestyle habits is an important first step in changing behaviour.

It is of course possible to lose weight in any way that cuts energy intake below energy needs. However, the crucial long term goal requires a more holistic approach focusing primarily on health and not unrealistic target body weight. Reducing dietary fat leads to a reduction in the risk of coronary heart disease; increasing complex carbohydrates helps promote a healthy gastrointestinal tract; higher intakes of fruit and vegetables may reduce the risk of some types of cancer. In addition, by eating a healthy, balanced diet a person is more likely to achieve and maintain a healthy weight.

So, tell your patients, friends, and relatives to throw away the fad diet books and start eating a healthy, balanced diet. The results might not be quick but at least it works in the long term.

Chapter 3

Body Modification and Cosmetic Surgery

Body Image and Conformity

Guinevere Turner

In the following article, Guinevere Turner examines why some people opt for cosmetic surgery to alter their bodies and others decorate their bodies with tattoos or body piercings. Although piercings and tattoos elicit more of a reaction in society than cosmetic surgery does, she argues that all body modifications stem from an individual's desire for attention. She concludes that people who get cosmetic surgery feel the need to conform to society's standards of beauty, while people with piercings strive to declare their originality to the world. Turner is an actress and screenwriter in Los Angeles, California.

If you had asked me when I was 13 if I wanted plastic surgery, I would have said, "Oh, my God. Fix everything. I'm so ugly and gross. Make me look like Brooke Shields, please!" I've changed a lot since then. Today, I wouldn't dream of having plastic surgery, if for no other reason than that my fear of surgery now outweighs my vanity (but only by a slim margin).

Ironically, though, I am both pierced and tattooed. What's more, I've had conversations with women with impossibly large

From "Modifying Our Bodies," by Guinevere Turner, *Advocate,* December 21, 1999.

breasts and slim noses who say, "Ouch! Didn't that hurt?" when they see my tongue piercing. I realize that we're coming from totally different places with our body modifications. I've now seen scars, botched jobs, and plastic surgery bills. But I take no high road here: I'm not rich, and I'm chicken.

Permanent Changes

My body modifications, which are less expensive and much quicker than most plastic surgeries, are nonetheless permanent and often more visible than plastic surgery at first glance. I'm sure my pierced tongue has elicited way more gasps than the average nose job, and people point to the tattoo on my foot much more than they would if I had fake breasts. So there's the difference: The surgery is meant to look real, natural, invisible, and the tattoos and piercings are meant to say, "Look at me, I'm a nonconformist!"

Let's backtrack. I got my tattoo, plain and simple, because I thought it would be a cool thing to do. I'm able to admit this now because my tattoo is faded and crappy-looking, and I curse the 17-year-old me who sat in Jim's Tattoo Shack on the Massachusetts–New Hampshire border saying, "Yeah, let's make it a fish."

My tongue piercing, well, that was different. It was seven years later, and I decided I was getting pretty straight-looking in my old age and that I needed a gay signifier, something to trigger gaydar, something that raised a sexuality-related eyebrow. I realize that this kind of thinking was equally lame. I'm just being honest here. However, it pretty much had the desired effect, but I was kind of cheating. You may not know this, but piercing your tongue has a high attention versus permanence ratio. It's all dramatic and rough-seeming, but the tongue is actually the fastest-healing tissue in the body. Twenty-four hours after you take it out, it heals up with little lasting

> We're coming from totally different places with our body modifications.

damage. Good thing for me too because now, six years later, the only symbolic message a tongue piercing gives is that you might be from the suburbs and be 14 to 19 years old.

Peer Pressure

In some ways it's all about peer pressure. I have a friend whose parents encouraged her to get a nose job when she was 15. Most of the other girls in her school already had one. She got tattoos instead and hid them from her parents. Now she's getting the tattoos lasered off, and her nose is intact. What does it all mean? It would seem that while on one level plastic surgery and tattooing/piercing stem from the same place, namely, a dissatisfaction with what you've been given, on another level they are opposites. Plastic surgery is born out of a need to conform (to society's ideas of what one should be) and tattooing/piercing evolves out of a need to announce one's nonconformity to the world. Although now plastic surgery can be pretty damn convincing, and tattoos are pretty easy to remove.

> Piercing your tongue has a high attention versus permanence ratio.

I'm reminded of the old Dr. Seuss story of the Star-bellied Sneeches. Some Sneeches had stars on their bellies, and some did not. The non-starred Sneeches invented a machine to make belly stars, and then the Star-bellied Sneeches invented a machine to take stars off, and soon nobody could figure out who was born with stars and who wasn't, and everyone was nice to each other.

I cast no stones. The need to conform and the need to stand out seem to me to stem from the same place. The way we choose to modify our bodies simply depends on whose attention we crave. I accidentally clamped down on my tongue piercing with my back teeth the other day and swallowed a piece of tooth. Not sexy. I took out the piercing and put it in my pocket, relieved that it was so easy to undo my particular conceit.

Body Piercing

Phaedra Thomas, Traci Brooks, Estherann Grace,
and Lara Hauslaib

According to Phaedra Thomas, Traci Brooks, Estherann
Grace, and Lara Hauslaib, people have been modifying
their bodies with piercings and tattoos since ancient times.
The authors contend that there are serious risks to body
piercing, and there is no sure way to prevent infection or
harm to your body. They suggest that if you decide to
pierce a part of your body, you should thoroughly research
the piercer and the salon before trusting your body to them.
They also describe the best way to clean your new piercing
and reduce the risk of infection. The authors are medical
professionals at the Center for Young Women's Health—
created by the Children's Hospital of Boston—which is
committed to improving the health and well-being of adolescent girls.

M any different cultures have pierced their bodies for centuries. If you look in a history book, you will find that
Egyptians, Greeks, and Romans did body art, such as piercing
and tattooing. People pierced their bodies for decoration to show
the person's importance in a group, or because they thought it
protected them from evil. Today, we know much more about the

risks of body piercing. Body piercing is a serious decision. Before you decide what you want to do, ask your friends, parents, and trusted adults what they think.

What Are Teens Saying About Body Piercing Today?

Ask other teens who have been pierced what they thought of the whole experience. How much did it cost? Was it painful? How long did it take to heal? If they had the chance to do it over again, would they?

Some tips teens have passed along to us:

• YOU do NOT have to pierce your body to "belong."

• YOU can ALWAYS change your mind or WAIT if you are not sure.

• If YOU do decide to have your body pierced, NEVER pierce your own body or let a friend do it because you can get very serious health problems.

What Are the Risks with Body Piercing?

The most serious risks are infections, allergic reactions, bleeding, and damage to nerves or teeth. Infections may be caused by hepatitis, HIV, tetanus, bacteria, and yeast. If the piercer washes his/her hands and uses gloves and sterile equipment and you take good care of your piercing, the risk of infection is lowered (but still exists).

> Body piercing is a serious decision.

Did you know that . . .

• You CAN get and/or spread a serious infection including HIV, if the piercing equipment hasn't been sterilized properly.

Infections caused by bacteria getting into the puncture of the piercing may also happen later, even after the piercing has healed.

• If the studio uses a piercing "gun" to do body piercings . . . LEAVE!! Piercing guns cannot be sterilized and should NOT be used for body piercing.

Another cause of problems from piercings is the wrong kind of jewelry for the area pierced. If the jewelry is too small, it can actually cut off the blood supply to the tissue, causing swelling and pain. If the jewelry is either too thin or too heavy or if you are allergic to the metal, your body can sometimes reject the jewelry (your body reacts against the jewelry because it is a "foreign object").

Know the Risks Before You Have Your Body Pierced

• Bacterial infection (where you had the piercing)
  • Excessive (a lot of) bleeding
  • Allergic reactions (especially to certain kinds of jewelry)
  • Damage to nerves (for example, you may lose feeling at the area that gets pierced)
  • Keloids (thick scarring at the piercing site)
  • Dental damage (swelling and infection of tongue, chipped and broken teeth, choking on loose jewelry)

Does It Matter Where on My Body I Get Pierced?

Healing time is different depending on where on your body you get pierced. Some places are more likely to get infected or have problems. Piercings on your ear lobes usually take about six to eight weeks to heal. But piercings on the side of your ear, which is cartilage, can take anywhere from 4 months to 1 year to heal. The reason for this is that the type of tissue in each area is different and the amount of pressure on the pierced area while you are sleeping is different.

Tongue piercings swell a lot at first but heal fairly quickly if the right type of jewelry is used. However, metal jewelry in the tongue piercing may damage gums and chip the enamel surface on your teeth. In fact, the ADA, which stands for the American Dental Association (a group of dentists that set professional standards for dentists in the United States), is against any type of oral piercings because of all the risks. In some cases, nipple piercings can damage some of the milk-producing glands in a young woman's breasts. This can cause infections or problems later if the woman decides to breast-feed her baby. Some pierced areas, like, navel (belly button) piercings, are more likely to become infected because of irritation from tight clothing. A pierced site needs air to help the healing process.

Where Should I Go?

You should ask friends and relatives with piercings where they went and if they liked the place. Look for a place that does a lot of piercings and that only employs piercers with piercing licenses. Some states make piercers get a license, while other states do not. So there are actually people who are doing body piercings with very little training! As you can imagine, this can be very dangerous for you. However, the APP, which stands for the Association of Professional Piercers (a professional organization of piercers), makes safety rules for people who do piercings. Make

> NEVER pierce your own body or let a friend do it.

sure that there is a certificate on the wall that says the piercer is registered with the APP. You may need to bring a copy of your birth certificate. If you are under eighteen years old, you will need your parents' or guardians' permission. Your parent/ guardian will need to go with you to the piercing salon and sign a consent form.

Since the law is different from state to state, you will need to find out what the law in your area says about whether or not you need parental permission to have a piercing.

What Should I Look For in a Piercing Salon?

When you go into a salon, look around. Is the place clean? The shop should be kept clean and sanitary. The lighting should be good so the piercers can see well while working. Do they wash their hands and use sterile gloves and instruments? All the instruments should either be brand new and disposable (meant to be thrown away after one use) or be sterilized in pouches. If the piercer uses disposable needles, you should see him/her open sealed packages of the needles! The piercers should throw away the needles in a biohazard container after using them.

What Kind of Jewelry Should I Buy?

It is best to use surgical stainless steel when you first have your piercing done. It is least likely to produce a foreign body reaction or infection in the skin. Other choices for when you first have your piercing done are metals like gold (AT LEAST 18k), titanium, or niobium. All of these cost more than surgical steel. For people who are extremely sensitive to metal, Teflon or nylon piercings may be used.

Look for a salon that has a large choice of jewelry. The salon should not tell you to use a certain type of jewelry just because it's the only kind they have.

What's Up with All the Different Kinds of Jewelry?

• Bars, which are the type of jewelry used in some piercings like the tongue, are measured in length (how long the bar is). When the piercing is first done, a longer bar will be used. When the piercing heals, a shorter bar is used.

• Ring jewelry is measured by diameter, or how wide the ring is.

• Gauge means the thickness of the jewelry. The smaller the gauge number, the thicker the jewelry. The APP says that jewelry no greater than 14 gauge should be used below the neck. This is because of the risk of a foreign body reaction and the possibility of the ring cutting the skin.

How Are Piercings Done?

An experienced piercer uses a hollow needle to create a hole by passing the needle through the body part you want pierced. The body jewelry is then inserted through the hole. Sometimes there can be a small amount of bleeding. You should not take aspirin or any pain medication that contains aspirin the week before any piercing is done, since these medicines may cause you to bleed a little bit more than usual. Remember, piercing guns should NEVER be used since it can damage tissue and cause infection.

How Much Will a Piercing Cost?

There are actually two costs with piercings—the site cost and the jewelry cost. The site cost depends on where on your body you get pierced. For example, ear and nose piercings usually cost less than tongue, nipple, or genital piercings. Gold jewelry costs more than stainless steel or another metal. You should shop around and check prices at different piercing salons before you decide on where to have your piercing done.

How Should I Clean My New Piercing?

1. Wash your hands first with soap and water before touching or cleaning the pierced area. (Don't let anyone else touch the pierced area until it is healed.)

2. Remove any crusty skin from the site and from the jewelry with warm water.

3. Gently wash the area around the piercing with antibacterial soap (liquid soap works the best).

4. Gently rinse off all of the soap and crusty discharge.

5. Gently dry the area with a paper towel or plain white napkin. (Bacteria can stay in cloth towels.)

6. Do steps 1–5 twice a day until the skin heals. (Over-washing or over-scrubbing can irritate the area.)

7. Do NOT use antibacterial ointments because they don't allow air to get to the area and they trap bacteria. . . .

Body piercing is a big decision. After understanding the risks, we hope that this information will help you make a decision that's best for you. If you do decide to get a body piercing, we hope that you will follow the guidelines in this information sheet. Go to a reliable salon/piercer, buy good jewelry, keep the site clean and away from irritating materials, and see your health care provider if you have symptoms of an infection!

I Got a Tattoo

Kristi L. Waterworth

In the following article, Kristi L. Waterworth describes her experience of getting a tattoo. She says that she got her tattoo because she was curious about the tattooing process, and it was a way for her to express her individuality. She recommends that if you decide to get a tattoo, get one that satisfies you and not your friends or family. She also suggests that you find a clean, reputable tattooing parlor and artist. Waterworth contributes to Teen Advice Online, an organization dedicated to providing support for teen problems through a network of peers from around the world.

O h my GOD! WHAT AM I DOING?
    I almost fainted as the tattoo artist, Hap, powered up his implement of destruction. At first, there was no pain at all. Then, it hit me.

Searing red lines of agony ran up and down the small butterfly design Hap was putting on my chest. The raw skin was becoming more sensitive by the second as he added colors and more lines.

I was on the verge of tears, and I was afraid, but he couldn't stop. He told me so. I glanced down at my chest, thinking maybe looking at it would help me conquer the pain.

From "Care and Feeding of Your New Tattoo," by Kristi L. Waterworth, www.teenadviceonline.org, 2001. Copyright © 2001 by Teen Advice Online. Reprinted with permission.

Blood spewed from every pore.

I almost threw up and I almost passed out at about the same time, but somehow, I managed to control myself.

It Was a Bargain

Relax, Kristi, this is the best buy you'll ever get. Only $45 for something that will last the rest of your life. You just can't beat a deal like that.

Then, suddenly, the machine stopped.

A blessing! A blessing from the Lord!

I looked the man straight in the face. "Is that it?"

"No, I have to go over it again."

I almost passed out in the chair. When the machine didn't start its melancholy buzz, I realized he was only messing with my head. Damn tattoo artists, anyway. They're such smart asses.

I paid Hap, glad to be free from his chamber of horrors. He gave me a paper with the proper feeding and maintenance of my newfound treasure. I was so happy! I think it was the endorphins.

Two hours later, I was sitting in my best friend's apartment, scolding myself for being tattooed. WHAT WERE YOU THINKING? ARE YOU MENTAL?

There was also an occasional "OUCH!" when I moved my arm the right way. When we pulled the gauze off, I was crying. I couldn't believe I had done such a strange thing just to satisfy my own curiosity. (My friend Kenna is a doctor-to-be, so she takes care of my bloody wounds, since I can't stand the stuff.) Anyway, she ripped the thing off as kindly as she could, all the while, I was bawling my eyes out. She took one look at the bloody piece of gauze.

> I was on the verge of tears, and I was afraid, but he couldn't stop.

"Look, Kristi, it's a butterfly!"

Through my tears, I almost died laughing.

Expressing Individuality

Now why did I feel the need to tell that story? Boredom? Just something for the world's youth who are thinking about tattooing every part of their bodies to read? Nah.

I was scared to death. I never had really known any "normal" tattooed people. I thought it would make me some kind of weirdo. But, I still had this insatiable curiosity that had only one cure. So after two years of deliberation, I went under the needle. And, looking back, I don't regret it. As a matter of fact, I'm

---

History of Tattoos

Throughout history tattooing and body piercing have been practiced by many cultures. The body of a 4,000-year-old tattooed man was discovered in a glacier on the Austrian border in 1992. Egyptians in the period from 4000 to 2000 B.C. identified tattooing with fertility and nobility. During the 17th and 18th centuries, European sailors traveling through the Polynesian islands saw extensive tattooing on both men and women. Since the 5th century B.C. the Japanese have used tattooing for ornamental, cosmetic, and religious purposes as well as for identification and punishment of criminals. In the late nineteenth century, tattooed royalty in England and European countries were fashionable. Lady Randolph Churchill (Winston's mother) had a snake tattooed around her wrist. . . .

In recent times tattoos have been most common among motorcyclists, criminals, gang members, individuals with psychiatric problems, and military personnel. Members of these groups often obtained tattoos to show loyalty to their group. Today the number of musicians and sports stars who are tattooed or body pierced has skyrocketed. Cher and Dennis Rodman are two of the most outspoken stars wearing tattoos. Many of these figures serve as role models for teenagers.

Barbara Freyenberger, *Iowa Health Book,* November 1998.

---

proud of it. I show it off as often as I can.

I guess this article isn't really as much about tattooing as it is about individuality versus ridicule. I'm sure there will be people I meet who will think less of me because I have it. I know my father would, so he doesn't know about it. He's a spend-thrift to the point of pain. The only things people in his little world need are food, clothing and a roof. There is no room for entertainment or curiosity. Those things must die with adulthood.

> I couldn't believe I had done such a strange thing just to satisfy my own curiosity.

So, to avoid the lecture that begins, "If you think you have so much money to waste, why don't you just move out?!?" followed by my mother having a nervous breakdown, he'll never know until I'm about 40. It's sad, but we do occasionally have to do those kinds of things to protect ourselves and others from unnecessary complications. But I digress.

Feeling Complete

In life, everyone has those things they have to do to be complete. Everyone has to do certain things that serve no real purpose other than to satisfy a long-standing curiosity. And, sometimes, that causes ridicule. There are a lot of people like my father living in the world right now. And that's ok, too. We need worker bees. If not for them, things would not run smoothly ever. They're the ones that leave dinner uneaten to drive 500 miles to repair a truck that's broken down on the road in the middle of nowhere. But, they're also the ones that do what is practical all of the time instead of most of the time.

Humans are just like animals. We need to play and to be curious and to wonder in order to exist successfully. We need these things to be healthy. So, I guess what I'm trying to say the long way is this: Don't worry what anyone else will think if you want to get a tattoo. It doesn't matter. Other people's feelings are irrelevant. The only person you have to live with the rest of your life is you. And if you've given it a lot of thought, it will enhance you because it'll be just like something that's always been there. It won't look funny or stand out ridiculously. However, I do want to give you a short list of guidelines to help you choose a parlor that is clean and will not give you more than you paid for (i.e., Hepatitis B, AIDS).

1. Look the place over WELL. If it looks clean and they don't seem annoyed by you asking questions about everything under God's green earth, it's a good sign.

2. Do some research. Find out where they advertise and who are the kinds of people that they target. If they shoot for middle-class, normal people, it's a good sign.

3. Look at the prices of the designs. If you can get anything worthwhile for under thirty bucks, I would worry. An experienced tattoo artist can make a killing with those things. They take next to no supplies (once the major equipment is purchased) and just a little bit of time.

4. See #1 and ASK A LOT OF QUESTIONS! Questions about the sterilization process and the application process are appropriate. Ask them if there will be a lot of blood and if that could pose a health risk. If they act cool and answer you in an honest and professional way, you're probably ok.

5. Be sure to get a Hepatitis screening if you suddenly start to feel sick or you notice anything weird going on with your body. Chances are, if you followed the above suggestions, you're going to be fine. But, if not, you need to know.

> Everyone has those things they have to do to be complete.

Ok, kiddos, I guess that's it. Just don't go running out and getting a tattoo for the wrong reasons. Don't just do it because your friends are, or because you haven't done an "18 and over" thing yet. Go to a dance club if you need an "18 and over" activity. Tattooing is not for the faint of heart (and you can't donate blood for a year afterwards).

I Lost My Daughter to Liposuction

Kathleen Marinelli

Recently, cosmetic surgery has become more common among young adults and teenagers. Because it is more common, however, some people forget that it is serious surgery with dangerous risks. In the following article, Kathleen Marinelli describes the death of her twenty-three-year-old daughter after a liposuction surgery. Marinelli insists that her daughter did not need liposuction, and she successfully sued the doctor for malpractice. If you decide to have cosmetic surgery, thoroughly research your surgeon and be aware of the health risks involved.

My daughter died after having plastic surgery she didn't even need. We wound up taking the case to court and winning, but that doesn't begin to make up for having lost my daughter. Lisa Marie was only 23 years old when she went to see Rami Geffner, M.D., in Toms River, because of a little rash on her face. Her HMO had suggested him as a dermatologist, but while she was in his waiting room, she read some pamphlets about the liposuction practice he also had. Lisa Marie was 5'2" and weighed only about 115 pounds. She worked out regularly

From "Pressure to Be Perfect," by Kathleen Marinelli as told to Deborah DiClementi, *Teen People*, April 1, 2001. Copyright © 2001 by People Weekly. Reprinted with permission.

and watched what she ate. But she felt that she had a little more fat on her thighs and legs than she wanted. During her appointment, she asked Dr. Geffner about liposuction, and he recommended that she have the procedure. When she told me what he'd said, I told her she didn't need the operation. But she and her fiance were planning a trip to Mexico and she said she wanted to look good in a bikini. She mulled it over and decided to do it.

Mother's Intuition

I'm a nurse assistant; I begged her to see another doctor, one who's supposed to be the best plastic surgeon in town. She agreed, but the other doctor couldn't see her for a while and she wanted the lipo right away. So she scheduled surgery with Dr. Geffner and went in for the preliminary blood work. I was worried about the doctor's qualifications, but she said, "Mom, I've come this far. I'm just going to have it done." Lisa Marie and I went to the mall together on the Saturday night before her surgery. She bought me a beautiful perfume bottle in the shape of a mother and daughter because Mother's Day was the next day. On that Sunday, Lisa Marie's older sister, Melissa, took her to Dr. Geffner's office. According to Melissa's court testimony, the surgery didn't go well. A nurse told her they had to keep stopping to give Lisa Marie more drugs because she said she could feel him running the suction tube in her inner thighs. Afterward, she was sent home with a prescription for a painkiller.

Lisa Marie went to bed, and the family checked on her throughout the night. The next morning she went to the kitchen for breakfast and had a seizure. Her younger sister, Suzanne, found her unconscious on the floor. We took her to the hospital, where, as I explained in court, they ran some tests but released her after a few hours, saying she must have had a reaction to the

> I was worried about the doctor's qualifications.

Making the Decision

Before a person decides to undergo cosmetic surgery for any reason, he or she needs to take the time to do some important homework. First, the reasons for wanting the surgery should be considered. "Undergo the surgery for yourself—and only for yourself," says Diana Barry, author of *Nips and Tucks: Everything You Must Know Before Having Cosmetic Surgery*. Barry points out that a best friend's opinion should not be the reason a person chooses cosmetic surgery.

Second, your expectations should be realistic. If a young woman is considering liposuction on her hips because she thinks it will make her more popular, that is not a realistic enough goal to warrant surgery.

Third, it is important to remember that any type of surgery carries risks. These issues should be thoroughly and frankly discussed with a doctor. Experts recommend choosing a doctor who is experienced in the procedure you are considering and is certified by the American Board of Medical Specialties as either a plastic surgeon, a dermatologist, or a dermatologic surgeon. Doctors should supply actual patient photos and give information about complications and follow-up care.

Melissa Abramovitz, *Current Health 2*, February 2001.

medication. As I was dressing her to take her home, she had another seizure and died right there. We later learned that a blood clot in one of her legs had traveled to a lung because Dr. Geffner had damaged a vein during liposuction and then tied her bandages too tightly, cutting off her circulation.

Court Ordeal

Two weeks after Lisa Marie's death, we filed a medical malpractice suit against the doctor that ultimately turned into an emotional four-year ordeal. In August 1998, the court found that

Dr. Geffner was responsible for Lisa Marie's death. We were granted only a little more than $500,000, which the court ordered him to pay. Our lawyer thought we should have gotten a much higher sum, but we didn't care. More than anything, we just wanted the public to know what had happened to our daughter. Incredibly, Dr. Geffner still has his license—although he says he no longer performs liposuctions. But I don't have my Lisa Marie.

Point of Contention: Should Teenagers Have Cosmetic Surgery?

According to the American Society of Plastic Surgeons, cosmetic operations on teenagers under the age of eighteen increased from 24,623 in 1998 to 306,384 in 2000. Some people argue that these figures represent a risky preoccupation with appearance among young people. Marianne, author of the website yestheyrefake.net, argues that surgically altering a body part can significantly improve a teenager's body image and level of confidence. On the other hand, Erin Schneweis, editor-in-chief of the *Kansas State Collegian*, contends that the risk factors of cosmetic surgery for teenagers, such as personal regret, infection, and surgical complications, outweigh the possible benefits, such as improved self-esteem. Both authors agree that cosmetic surgery is a serious decision with definite risks.

Cosmetic Surgery Is Okay for Teenagers

Marianne

When I was in junior high and high school I remember the awkwardness of being a teen, the low self-esteem that can be experienced whilst "coming of age" and the cruel comments directed at others. For many of us, these comments burn a permanent place into our minds and remain with us for the rest of our lives. These comments can make us feel bad about ourselves even if there is no reasoning or fact that brought the offending comment on in the first place. During this time of personal growth, what people think of us really *does* matter. It doesn't end there, either; you carry that responsibility to represent a positive image for the rest of your life. Your parents had to bathe and comb their hair and dress well for work, as did their parents. In fact, most places of employment will not tolerate an unwashed, shabby and generally offensive appearance. Should this really matter? Ideally, no—*but it does.* Of course, combing your hair and having a rhinoplasty [nose job] are two different things—but if one gives you better self-confidence, and it isn't hurting another—what's the problem?

It is ignorant to think that we shouldn't care if another disapproves or comments on our appearance. If there were no preference, and no one cared about appearance—we would still be running around smelly, overly hairy, and wearing the rotting traces of clothing with a big stick as an accessory—not to mention the population would be less. Humans are never satisfied, which leads to growth. Growth leads to progress. And so on. That is why social acceptance creates quite an impact during these important growth years. Teens see that their parents and society in general prefer certain aesthetic criteria, so how can teenagers be expected to overlook the desire to look their best when they see it all around them every day? It isn't a case of *monkey see, monkey do*—it's about reality. How can we not feel as if we must conform to society's ideal? We are bombarded by the beautiful everywhere we go; and it is hypocritical to say "do as I say, not as I do." The fact is that social development during the teen years is a powerful thing, and even though having low self-esteem can have many underlying factors, sometimes these issues are purely aesthetic.

Regardless of what another thinks, one should never, ever change himself or herself into something else, either aesthetically or emotionally, for someone else or to make others like them. Do what makes *you* happy. You must make yourself happy, and as long as it doesn't hurt anyone (including yourself), why should someone else care what . . . you do? . . .

Where to Draw the Line

Some issues like insecurity or mental and emotional issues should be noted when deciding whether a procedure should even be entertained. If you are doing this for someone else—that is a big red flag. If you are under the impression that a cosmetic procedure will solve all of your issues—it won't. You remain the same person that you would be with the former version of your body. It won't change who you are, and it won't make someone like you.

Many teens feel as if they must conform to the thin, waif-like bodies of runway models and cover girls. I can relate to this, as I had a minor eating disorder when I was in my teens. This is a serious issue—please, please, please seek counseling if you are obsessed about your body weight, food, or eating to the point of unhealthiness. Also, obsessing over yourself at *any* age is very damaging. Liposuction is not usually appropriate for a teenager so eating healthy and exercising may help. If not, underlying hormonal or thyroid problems may exist, so be sure to consult with your physician. And if after

> It is ignorant to think that we shouldn't care if another disapproves or comments on our appearance.

all this, stubborn pockets of fat at the gender or genetic specific areas still exist in late adolescence, liposuction is *sometimes* considered. . . .

Will My Friends Be Able to Tell?

Some concerns of many of you may be things like, will my friends be able to tell? Will they care? Will they make fun of me? etc. You can either choose to tell them or not, quite frankly it is no one's business but yours or your parents'. Not everyone is so blatant and loud as I am about cosmetic surgery. In California, nose casts aren't that big of a deal. In high school it is

> One should never . . . change himself or herself into something else.

quite the norm to have a septoplasty/rhinoplasty (nose job) during the school year much less over summer vacation. The bruising of a septoplasty/rhinoplasty is pretty much gone in 8–10 days, the swelling will diminish over the next few weeks, and quite frankly, if you have the surgery over summer vacation, by the time you go back to school no one will ever know; unless of course the change is dramatic, like a jaw advancement, severe hump, or prominent nose. The definition following a rhinoplasty is so very gradual that not even most daily acquaintances will notice. The only way to tell is to compare photos. Besides, a septoplasty is more functional than a rhinoplasty—which is mostly for cosmetic applications. Septoplasty is often covered by insurance.

You can address the issue [with your friends] early on as to not cause drama. Or you can keep quiet and never let them in on it. If they find out later, nip it in the bud, and either tell them about it or let them know that you feel it is none of their business. Sometimes hiding things causes more curiosity though, so be careful. And never lie if it will be uncovered later. It only makes you look guilty and ashamed. Lying and not disclosing something are two different things. Besides, if they are your friends, why would they care—they just may have cosmetic concerns themselves. Besides, don't ever think that it is shallow or vain to care about what you look like. Don't let anyone tell you different either; if that were so we would never brush our hair, put on makeup or shave. *Looking* good makes us *feel* good; where's the shame in that? . . .

Risks of Cosmetic Surgery and Noninvasive Procedures

All surgery has risks and even acne treatment has its own cautions. Please read each and every bit of information you can find on a subject (unless it's redundant) before deciding if it is worth it to you or not. . . .

Please discuss with your surgeon the risks and complications [of cosmetic surgery] and if he fails to mention any risks, run, don't walk from his office. . . . This is very important! Complications do arrive and one must be fully prepared in the event of a negative reaction or result. . . .

> It is ignorant to think that we shouldn't care if another disapproves or comments on our appearance.

Don't think for a minute that if you are attractive the world will fall at your feet—the shallow and ignorant may, but truly there is much more to life than looks.

From "Cosmetic Enhancement 4 Teens," by Marianne, www.yestheyrefake. net, December 10, 2001. Copyright © 2001 by Enhancement Media. Reprinted with permission.

Cosmetic Surgery May Be Harmful to Teenagers

Erin Schneweis

Too many people are making themselves into human Mr. Potato Heads. The fountain of youth now is equipped with a human fat flowbee [a hair cutting apparatus that is attached to a vacuum cleaner] and silicone pillows.

We are in a world of lifting, tucking, suctioning and implanting.

According to the American Society for Aesthetic Plastic Surgery, there were 5.7 million cosmetic surgical and non-surgical procedures performed in 2000. Baby boomers, people between the ages of 35 to 50, accounted for 43 percent of that figure. The second highest group was 19- to 34-year-olds, who accounted for 25 percent of the patients.

In 1999, American plastic surgeons performed nearly 822,000 facelifts, eyelid surgeries, breast augmentations, liposuctions and tummy tucks. Women accounted for 728,000 of that figure.

Unrealistic Expectations

I wonder how many of those women went in looking like Bea Arthur with expectations of leaving looking like Britney Spears. On the other hand, I would place money there are a lot of teen-aged girls who have had cosmetic surgery and then ended up regretting their choices. Some of them probably wish they would have left their bodies the way they were made instead of trying to create a new image.

Granted, cosmetic surgery has improved, but there still are great risks involved, such as excessive bleeding, infection, surgical complications, injury to the wound after surgery and heavy scarring.

The question no longer is what can be fixed, but more importantly—what can't be?

Short-Order Surgeries

It is similar to a fast-food place. I can just picture a gum-smacking, beehive-wearing old lady, asking, "Did you want your breasts enlarged with implants or the lift? For a few extra thousand, you can get those reconstructed.

"Oh, you want the number four? That's the tummy tuck, eyebrow transplant and the power cannula liposuction. Now, with the lipo did you want the liposculpture or liposhaving? And did you want that mini-sized?"

In middle school, you weren't cool unless you had designer jeans. Did you know they have designer vaginas? Nothing like a Gucci É. You get the point.

For those men out there who aren't equipped like a rented donkey from Mexico or Dirk Diggler [from the movie "Boogie Nights"],

> The fountain of youth is now equipped with a human fat flowbee and silicone pillows.

there are penile extensions offered. In the October 2001 issue of *Maxim,* it states this type of surgery, along with the widening, can cost a minimum of $9,000. Imagine if the surgeon accidentally thought you wanted a reduction.

Temporary Fixes

Even though I am using humor, there can be such serious complications for these surgeries.

These surgeries only offer temporary fixes.

Underneath the silicone, the facelifts and the new physical image, a fragile self-esteem still might exist.

When a person is involved in an accident, reconstructive surgery is acceptable. It is fair for the individual to change his or her image after a negative experience has altered it.

There also is a difference between someone who gets one thing done versus trying to change his or her whole image.

Flawed Beauty

Beauty is found in imperfections. It is what separates people and makes them interesting. Our natural scars tell stories. The lines on our faces are from laughter. True beauty cannot be store-bought.

It is a shame we are so focused on our physical appearance we forget about so many other important things. Instead of reading classic novels, some read only plastic surgery pamphlets. And it shows. Some are too busy trying to defy time, and they end up wasting their lives under the knife.

As much fun as the game "What's real and what's fake?" can be, it shows the overall lack of acceptance.

While it might be entertaining for Mr. Potato Head to try new looks, underneath it all, he still is just a potato.

From "Cosmetic Surgery Can Be Harmful," by Erin Schneweis, *Kansas State Collegian*, October 24, 2001. Copyright © 2001 by Kansas State Collegian. Reprinted with permission.

Chapter 4

How to Improve
Your Body Image

Accept Your Body

Cindy Maynard

According to Cindy Maynard, teenagers are bombarded with messages that stress society's obsession with physical perfection. She claims that teenagers pick up cues from their families, friends, and the media about beauty, and they use those cues to judge whether they are attractive. Maynard contends that many of these messages are damaging to young people's self-image because most of the images in the media are unrealistic; girls covet the abnormally thin bodies of fashion models, and boys emulate the steroid-induced bulk of body-builders. She maintains that teenagers must learn to accept their bodies as they are and strive to be healthy rather than perfect. Maynard is a medical writer and nutritional counselor and therapist.

In this world of super-hunks and airbrushed beauties, finding fault with normal bodies has become a national pastime. Here's how to hold your head high and think the best of yourself—whatever your body's shape.

Negative Body Image

Many teens suffer from what the experts call "negative body image"—they don't like their bodies. And they're letting their thoughts about their bodies shatter their self-esteem, their sense of how valuable they are as people.

"I find it impossible to ever be satisfied with my body," says Sarah, a high school senior from San Diego, California. "After each pound slips away, I still feel the need to be thinner."

Her friend Stephanie understands Sarah's dilemma. "All I see are models in magazines who look so perfect, and that's how I want to be," she says.

Sarah and Stephanie are not alone. Nearly two of every five teens who replied to a nationwide survey that appeared in *USA Weekend* in 1997 said they would feel better about themselves if they lost weight or (among boys) bulked up. The survey, published in May 1998, discovered that nearly seven out of 10 respondents said they felt either "somewhat satisfied" or "not at all satisfied" with their looks.

Tony, 14, probably would agree. "I feel sad because everyone calls me fat," he says. "I exercise and do push-ups to help me lose weight. The kids call me 'Fat Boy,' 'Fatso,' and stuff—and it makes me mad."

Sarah, Stephanie, and Tony take part in a weekly body image group held for adolescents at Mesa Vista Hospital in San Diego. They asked to be identified by first name only. The group began when teens expressed a need to discuss their feelings and perceptions about their bodies in a supportive forum.

> [Teens are] letting their thoughts about their bodies shatter their self-esteem.

Mirror, Mirror

In this media-driven age, it seems most people are dissatisfied with their bodies. Recent studies show that kids as early as third grade are concerned about their weight. But, with body shapes rapidly changing, teens are the most vulnerable. During teen years, there is a lot of pressure to fit in. . . .

Girls, in general, tend to be overly concerned about weight

and body shape, say psychologists. Many strive for the "perfect" body and judge themselves by their looks, clothes, and ability to stay cover-girl thin.

But boys don't escape, either. Today's culture celebrates tough, muscular, and well-sculpted males. So naturally, boys are concerned with the size and strength of their body. They think they have to be "real" men. Yet many admit being confused as to what's expected of them. This confusion can make it harder than ever to feel good about themselves. It's not surprising that sports such as wrestling, boxing, and gymnastics—which demand top conditioning—can contribute to a negative body image. The need to make weight for a sport often leads to eating problems.

> Girls . . . tend to be overly concerned about weight and body shape.

But boys like Jon Maxwell, 15, say sports make them feel better about themselves. "Guys are in competition, especially in the weight room," Jon says. "One will say, 'I can bench 215 pounds,' and the other guy says, 'Well, I can bench 230 pounds.' If you're stronger, you're better." Daniel Schaufler, age 16, agrees. "Guys are into having the perfect body," he says. "[And] if you feel good about your body, you automatically feel good about yourself."

Mission Impossible

Most of our cues about what we should look like come from the media, parents, and peers. This constant obsession with weight, the size of our body, and longing for a different shape or size can be painful.

Most teens watch an average of 22 hours of TV a week and are deluged with images of fat-free bodies in the pages of health, fashion, and teen magazines, according to Eva Pomice in her book, *When Kids Hate Their Bodies*. The result: Many try to achieve this "look," which is an impossible goal. A female should look like and have the same proportions as Barbie or Kate Moss, and a male should look like Arnold Schwarzenegger? As a result, many teens intensely dislike their bodies.

Take a look at the most popular magazines on the newsstands. Psychologist David M. Garner says in a recent *Psychology Today* article: "The media show an image of the perfect woman that is unattainable for somewhere between 98 and 99 percent of the female population." Remember: It's a career for these women; they're pros. Many have had major body makeovers and have full-time personal trainers. Photos in ads can be airbrushed or changed by computer. Body and facial imperfections, such as pimples, can be erased or changed at will.

The images of men and women in ads today have the power to make us feel bad about, and lose touch with, ourselves. Ads aren't intended to promote self-esteem or positive self-image. They're intended to sell products—and they do. In the United States, consumers spend billions of dollars to pursue the perfect body. The message "thin is in" is blasted at us thousands of times a day through TV, movies, magazines, billboards, newspapers, and songs. In a 1997 Body Image Survey, published by *Psychology Today,* teenagers reported that viewing very thin or muscular models made them feel insecure about themselves.

> Ads aren't intended to promote self-esteem or positive self-image.

Parents can give mixed messages, too—especially if they're constantly dieting or have body or food issues of their own. How young people perceive and internalize these childhood messages about their bodies determines their ability to be confident about their appearance.

Slimming Down, Bulking Up

America's preoccupation with dieting has made the diet business a multibillion-dollar industry. And it put questionable diet drugs, such as fen-phen, on the market. Fenfluramine (Pondimin and Redux) diet pills were taken off the market in 1997 because of their link to heart damage.

Just as bad, some student athletes who want to build strength are using dangerous anabolic steroids or other hormones. These chemicals have serious side effects, and they can stunt growth and cause liver damage, cancer, and high blood pressure.

> Student athletes who want to build strength are using dangerous anabolic steroids or other hormones.

This intense focus on food, fat, and body building also can lead to abnormal eating habits—such as yo-yo dieting and compulsive eating—that can turn into eating disorders.

Eating disorders, such as anorexia and bulimia, aren't new. More than 100 years ago, the first case of anorexia nervosa, or self-induced starvation, was documented. The incidence of eating disorders, including compulsive overeating and dieting, continues to increase. The American Psychiatric Association (APA) estimates that at any given time 500,000 Americans are battling eating disorders.

These disorders hit males and females in every area of society. More people became aware of them in 1995 when Princess Di began talking openly about her struggles with bulimia.

Christy Henrich, a high-ranked gymnast, paid the highest price. At the time of her death, she was 22 years old and weighed barely 50 pounds. Actress Tracey Gold still struggles with her eating disorder.

Body Image, Body Love

Psychologists and counselors recognize that a negative body image has a powerful impact on self-esteem, our assessment of our value as individuals. When we think about body image, generally we think about aspects of our physical appearance.

But body image is much more. It is our mental picture of our

bodies as well as of our thoughts, feelings, judgments, sensations, awareness, and behavior. It's part of our mental picture of
our total selves—the picture that shapes the way we think about
our value as people.

Feel bad about your body, in other words, and in time you're
likely to feel bad about other aspects of yourself. It's not un-
common for people who think poorly of their bodies to have
problems in other areas of their lives—including relationships
and careers. That's why it's so important, experts say, to avoid
letting your body affect your self-esteem. Positive self-esteem,
says the National Mental Health Associ-
ation (NMHA), "means you really like
yourself a lot, both inside and out . . .
how you look as well as what you believe in."

> Feel bad about your body . . . and in time you're likely to feel bad about other aspects of yourself.

Iris, age 18, who is currently at Mon-
tecatini, a residential treatment center
for anorexia in La Costa, California, is working to raise her self-
esteem. "I must work hard to keep my chin up, establish eye
contact, and have the courage, honesty, and trust to say what I
am feeling," she says. "I have a right to be heard and to give my
opinion. That is one way I will accomplish self-respect and gain
the same respect from others."

But you don't have to have an eating disorder to find achieving a healthy self-image a challenge. Here are some tips from
the NMHA and elsewhere on how teens who are unhappy with
their bodies can start feeling better about themselves.

Accepting Your Body

How can you learn to feel good and accept yourself no matter
what your size or shape?

First step: When you look in the mirror, make sure you find at
least one good point for every demerit you give yourself. Become aware of your positives.

Here are some other steps you can take to build a better body image—and more positive self-esteem:

- Accept the fact that your body's changing. In the teen years, your body is a work in progress. Don't let every new inch or curve throw you off the deep end.
- Decide which of the cultural pressures—glamour, fitness, thinness, media, peer group—prevent you from feeling good about yourself. Then do something to counteract this. How about not buying magazines that promote unrealistic body images?
- Exercise. When you want to feel good about the way you look, exercise. It helps improve your appearance, health, and mood.
- Emphasize your assets. You have many. Give yourself credit for positive qualities. If there are some things you want to change, remember: Self-discovery is a lifelong process.
- Make friends with the person you see in the mirror. Say "I like what I see. I like me." Do it until you believe it.
- Question ads. Instead of saying "What's wrong with me?" say "What's wrong with this ad?" Write the company. Set your own standards instead of letting the media set them for you.
- Ditch dieting and the scale. These are two great ways to develop a healthy relationship with your body and weight.
- Challenge size bigotry and fight size discrimination whenever you can. Don't speak of yourself or others with phrases like "fat slob" or "thunder thighs."
- Be an example to others by taking people seriously for what they say, feel, and do rather than how they look.

Accepting yourself is the starting point. Monique, age 18, in treatment for an eating disorder in La Costa, California, says she has learned to feel better about her body and herself. She has become more appreciative of those "inner qualities that make up who I am, such as my creativity, my intuition, and my self-motivation." At the same time, she has learned to block out "the negative thoughts based on my distorted body image, such as being too fat, never good enough for anyone, including myself."

You can't exchange your body for a new one. The best you can do is find peace with the one you have. Your body is where you're going to be living for the rest of your life. Isn't it about time you made it your home?

A Healthy Lifestyle Can Improve Your Body Image

Kathiann M. Kowalski

According to Kathiann M. Kowalski, teenagers are busier with schoolwork, sports, extracurricular activities, family obligations, and jobs than they have ever been. She contends that this fast-paced lifestyle leads many teenagers to indulge in high-fat and high-calorie foods, such as hamburgers and pizza, and neglect healthier foods, like fruits and vegetables. These poor eating habits, combined with a lack of regular exercise, may contribute to negative self-image because they result in unhealthy bodies. She maintains that eating healthy foods, including plenty of fruits and vegetables, and regular exercise can improve body image. Kowalski is a contributor to *Current Health 2*, a monthly journal that contains information about nutrition, fitness, personal health, drugs, and other health issues for teenagers.

Millions of American teens are overweight, while others are literally starving themselves. What's going on? Here's how what you eat affects your health.

From "Fuel or Fixation: What Role Does Food Play in Your Life?" by Kathiann M. Kowalski, *Current Health 2*, December 2000. Copyright © 2000 by Weekly Reader Corporation. Reprinted with permission.

Classmates called David "Beluga Boy" and other nasty names. He'd been overweight for years. When he was in sixth grade, he was 5'3" tall and weighed 145 pounds.

Meanwhile, Gina wanted the perfect dancer's body. Afraid of being fat, the 5'8" girl ate hardly anything. When she finally collapsed and was admitted to the hospital, she weighed just 99 pounds. Doctors diagnosed her eating disorder as anorexia nervosa.

Why does food have such opposite effects on teens' lives?

Supersize

The U.S. Department of Agriculture (USDA) estimates that 4.7 million school-age children and teens in America are overweight. That's about 10 percent of the total. Being overweight is defined as having a body mass index (BMI) greater than the 95th percentile for a person's age and height. Other teens aren't overweight or underweight, but they don't eat a healthy diet either. One-sixth of American students' diets don't meet the dietary standards of the USDA Food Guide Pyramid.

Teens' hectic schedules contribute to poor eating habits and nutrition. Most teens struggle with trying to balance schoolwork, sports practices, club meetings, family responsibilities, part-time jobs, volunteering, and social activities. Constantly on the run, many teens eat whatever takes the least effort—whether at home or not. Sit-down restaurant portions generally contain more fat than home-cooked meals. Fast-food meals are often "just" a burger with fries or several slices of pizza. Calories and fat pile up.

> Teens' hectic schedules contribute to poor eating habits and nutrition.

While teens on the whole are busier than ever, they're becoming less active physically. When teens fail to take time for regular exercise, a sedentary lifestyle can lead to weight problems. Too much extra weight causes physical ailments. Short-term problems include a lack of energy, headaches, and difficulty concentrating. According to the USDA, long-term problems include a higher risk for heart disease, diabetes, and stroke. In fact, type 2 adult-onset diabetes is now showing up among children and teens.

Mirror, Mirror on the Wall

Many overweight teens have poor body images. In one study by University of Minnesota researchers, 91 percent of overweight girls and 75 percent of overweight boys were unhappy with their weight. More startling were the percentages of non-overweight teens who were unhappy: 58 percent and 31 percent, respectively.

> It's important to have a good, healthy mental outlook regardless of what your weight is.

Why so much dissatisfaction? Page through any teen magazine or watch most prime-time TV shows, and the media's image of beauty becomes clear. Attractive young women are generally portrayed as slender and tall. Attractive guys are usually muscular. As if this weren't enough, many fitness articles expressly tell young women that weight loss will make them more attractive. Guys are urged to beef up their bodies. At the same time that these images are being reinforced, young adolescents' bodies are undergoing important changes. Girls naturally gain body fat during puberty as their bodies prepare for menstruation. Boys may have their growth spurts before their bodies build muscle mass. These rapid physical changes may make teens feel awkward.

Ironically, the "ideal" woman and man portrayed in the media are so rare, they almost don't exist. The media set up images that fool viewers and readers into thinking that many people are like models, when in reality, the average American woman weighs 140 pounds and is 5'4" tall, reports Eating Disorders and Prevention, Inc. In contrast, the typical model is 5'11" and weighs 117 pounds. That makes the model thinner than 98 percent of American women. Such unrealistic images place enormous pressures on young people. When teens feel they can't measure up, their self-esteem suffers. And that can put a damper on everything. In her book *Wake Up, I'm Fat,* actress Camryn Manheim recalls years of unhappiness as an overweight teen.

Aiming for the supposed ideal body, some teens turn to severe diets. They cut out all carbohydrates, drastically cut calories, or eat only certain types of food. Initial weight loss is mostly loss of water or muscle that the body needs. Any other weight lost often creeps back later when teens can't keep up the fad diet's strict rules and requirements. Then they feel even more frustrated.

Still other teens develop eating disorders. Obsessed by the fear of being fat, some teens literally starve themselves to death. Others eat compulsively whenever they feel stressed, depressed, or even just bored.

Build Up Your Body Image

With a distorted view of food's role in their lives, some teens mistakenly expect that losing weight will make everything in their lives better. But thin people have problems too, says Keith Ayoob, a nutritionist at the Albert Einstein College of Medicine. Ayoob says, "It's important to have a good, healthy mental outlook regardless of what your weight is."

> The government's Dietary Guidelines include a recommendation . . . to get at least 30 minutes of physical activity daily.

How can you develop a healthy outlook? First, be glad that everyone differs from the "ideal" in some way. People have different shapes and body types. People with ectomorph body types have naturally slender, reedy shapes. In contrast, people with endomorph body types naturally tend to store more fat throughout their bodies. That gives them a softer, rounder physique. People with mesomorph body types naturally tend to build up muscle mass, even without long hours in the gym. Add in variations in height, skin tone, eye color, hair color, and other features, and you get the wonderful diversity that makes up America.

Next, take inventory. Write down at least five good things about yourself. As you think of more positives, add them to the list. Then, think about people you admire: athletes, civic leaders, teachers, humanitarians, entertainers, and others. Chances are, few or none of them look like movie stars or models. Heroes don't stand around looking in the mirror all day. They're people who do things.

Eating the Right Stuff

Although surveys show that children and teens know the basics of good nutrition, many young people (as well as adults) do not apply that information to their daily lives.

As a result, sugar and fats dominate the diet of many teens, says the Center for Science in the Public Interest. Sugar (usually in the form of soda and junk food) makes up 25 percent of the diet of most teens, and fats also can contribute a lot of calories—up to 50 percent of many teens' diet. It's no wonder then that more than 20 percent of teens are overweight. And if you're overweight in adolescence, you have an 80 percent chance of turning into an overweight adult.

"Fat," of course, is a label no one likes. But, according to the Centers for Disease Control (CDC), teens should be more upset over the long-term health risks of obesity: increased risk of early death, heart disease, diabetes, gallbladder disease, joint disease and arthritis, and some cancers.

Janice Arenofsky, *Current Health 2*, May 1997.

Being active is a sure way to put thoughts about your weight, eating, and body image into their proper perspective. Do things that fit with your ultimate goals. Find out about colleges and possible careers. Invest energy in your schoolwork. Make plans for yourself and follow through.

Do things with friends. If those things involve more than sitting or eating, so much the better! Friends share challenges and experiences with you. And real friends like you just the way you are.

Do things for other people by volunteering in your community. Helping others out of genuine concern will almost certainly make you feel better about yourself.

Finally, do things for fun. The government's Dietary Guidelines include a recommendation for both adults and children to get at least 30 minutes of physical activity daily. So, instead of staring at the TV or computer screen, get out for a hike or bike ride. Get friends together to shoot some hoops. Go for a swim. An active lifestyle will help you stay healthy. And feeling good physically lets you appreciate your body.

Get a Second Opinion

Beyond this, stop asking yourself, "Do I look fat?" One recent study in *Pediatrics and Adolescent Medicine* reported that only about 10 percent of teens were actually overweight, and another 14 percent were "borderline." Despite that, more than 50 percent of teen girls and 25 percent of teen boys said they were overweight when they were not. Translation: You may not be the best person to judge. Instead, ask your doctor or a dietitian. He or she can help determine your body mass index.

If you're overweight, decide what you want to do. Losing weight is OK, says Ayoob, "but you want to do it safely and with health in mind. . . ." Moreover, what constitutes a healthy weight varies for each teen. "It doesn't always mean conforming to what the charts say you should weigh," stresses Ayoob. Body frame, medical history, family traits, and other issues are factors to be considered.

What You Eat Counts

Whether their weight is heavy, low, or normal, almost all teens can improve their diets. "In particular," says Ayoob, "most teen diets are woefully lacking in fruits, vegetables, and low-fat dairy products."

To figure out what you should be eating, check the USDA's Food Guide Pyramid. Whole grains, fruits, and vegetables should form the bulk of your diet. Add in protein and low-fat dairy products, and use sweets and fats sparingly.

To keep track of calories and particular nutrients, use the Nutrition Facts labels found on most food products. Pay attention to the serving size, and over the course of the day, try to stay at or under 100 percent of the Daily Values for fat, saturated fat, cholesterol, and sodium.

Conversely, try to get at least 100 percent of the Daily Value for fiber, vitamins, and minerals.

Since your bones are still growing, aim for 130 percent of the Daily Value for calcium. That's roughly four servings of low-fat dairy products.

Don't fear that you'll have to spend hours preparing food or survive on just bean sprouts and brown rice. "Eating healthfully can be easy and also really enjoyable," says Ayoob. "Any foods that adolescents like can fit in." If you like ice cream or pizza, that's fine. Just watch the portion size. And make sure other low-fat nutritious choices throughout the day balance out any of your indulgences.

Healthy eating is easier when you have lots of variety, so plan ahead to give yourself convenient choices. Stock up on portable foods such as fresh fruit, low-fat string cheese, hard-boiled eggs, single-serve applesauce cups, bagels, whole-grain breads, and containers of milk, juice, or water. Even if you're running late, you can still grab a quick breakfast of milk, grapes, and half a bagel.

Moderation, balance, and variety are key. Instead of obsessing about being on a diet, enjoy tasty foods that give you the nutrition you need. Let healthy eating habits provide the fuel for your active lifestyle.

Proper Nutrition Can Improve Your Body Image

Jenna A. Bell-Wilson

According to Jenna A. Bell-Wilson, teens and their parents are misinformed about a teenager's nutritional requirements. As a result, many teenagers are overweight or unhealthy and suffer poor body image. In the following article, Bell-Wilson articulates the amount of calories, vitamins, and minerals growing teenagers need to stay healthy and active. She maintains that adequate nutrition and regular exercise improve teens' health and, subsequently, their body image. Bell-Wilson is a registered dietitian and a consultant at the New Mexico Sports and Wellness and Southwest C.A.R.E. Center and is an e-counselor for www.Dietwatch.com, an online diet and health forum.

The teen years can be filled with tumultuous physical, emotional and intellectual growth. Today's teens are barraged by media images showing them what clothes they should wear, what music they should listen to and even what foods they should eat. Fast-food restaurants and soft-drink ads target adolescents and entice them with images of happy, slim teens enjoying unhealthy products. Anxious to declare their independence from their parents, teens often adapt poor eating habits, snatching meals on the run. This could not happen at a more inopportune time, since proper nutrition during the teen years is crucial for growth and sets the stage for healthy eating habits that last a lifetime.

Recent studies have underscored just how vulnerable and misinformed teens are. The National Health and Nutrition Examination Survey of 1999 found that 14 percent of adolescents ages 12 to 19 are overweight (body mass index above the 85th percentile), while the U.S. Youth Risk Behavior Surveillance Survey of 1999 revealed that 16 percent are at risk for becoming overweight. At the same time, more than 58 percent of the 1,270 participants in the Youth Risk Behavior Surveillance Survey said they had been attempting to control their weight during the 30 days preceding the survey and more than 12 percent reported going without food for more than 24 hours to lose weight. Additionally, under 24 percent of these same participants consumed the recommended five servings of fruits and vegetables per day, and a mere 18 percent consumed three or more glasses of milk per day. Statistics like these underscore the need to educate teens about healthy nutrition practices and provide practical strategies for parents responsible for feeding their busy adolescents. . . .

> Anxious to declare their independence from their parents, teens often adapt poor eating habits, snatching meals on the run.

Nutrient and Energy Needs

The Recommended Dietary Allowances (RDA) and the Dietary Reference Intakes (DRI) indicate average nutrient needs for adolescent boys and girls. These estimates can be limited in usefulness, however, because they do not take into account an individual's stage of physical maturity.

Energy needs for growing adolescents vary tremendously, depending on gender, rate of growth and stage of development. The RDA is 2,200 calories per day for adolescent girls and 2,500 to 3,000 calories per day for their male peers. However, more active teens require more calories. For example, an active 15-year-old boy may need over 4,000 calories per day.

The following sections describe some of the basic nutrients that teens of both genders need for proper development but often do not get in the correct amounts. Also listed are whole-food sources that contain these nutrients, are readily available and are likely to appeal to most teens.

Pumping Iron

Iron needs are great among all teenagers, both male and female. Boys require a diet high in iron because of their increase in muscle mass and subsequent increase in blood volume. Girls need to increase their iron intake upon onset of menses. For 11- to 15-year-old girls, the RDA for iron is 15 grams (g) per day; for boys in the same age range, it is 12 g per day.

Excellent sources of iron include meat, poultry and fish. Although iron can also be found in enriched cereals, beans, spinach and fortified soy products, these foods contain compounds that can impair iron absorption. One way to increase absorption is to eat these foods in conjunction with other items that are high in vitamin C (e.g., tomatoes, oranges, strawberries, green peppers, broccoli and romaine lettuce).

> Iron needs are great among all teenagers, both male and female.

Dried fruits and raisins are also good sources of iron, as they are often dried in iron pans! Iron supplements are not recommended for teenagers, because the iron in supplements is much less absorbable than the iron in whole foods. However, supplementation may be warranted if a physician determines through testing that iron stores are inadequate, which is common in teens who consume a strict vegetarian diet.

Boning Up on Calcium

Calcium is another nutrient that is often in short supply in teens. Calcium intake directly influences the density, length and width of bone, as well as the achievement of peak bone mass. During the teen years, not only is the need for calcium higher, but the ability to absorb and retain calcium is much greater. Almost 91 percent of the adult skeletal volume is formed by age 17. The risk of developing osteoporosis later in life can be affected by the amount of bone mass attained during the teen years.

> Calcium intake directly influences the density, length and width of bone.

Despite their immense need for calcium, adolescents consume far less than the required 1,300 milligrams per day. Teenage girls are especially vulnerable, as research has shown that their consumption of calcium-rich milk products decreases during adolescence. This decline may be related in part to increased consumption of soft drinks.

Readily available calcium sources for teens include low-fat milk, yogurt and cheese; puddings; and soy products. Teens on the go can up their calcium intake by simply grabbing a slice of string cheese or a container of yogurt.

Protein (or Pro-Teen)

While many vital nutrients are in short supply in the teenage diet, protein typically is not. In fact, a 1995 study of 3,350 adolescents found that most consumed more than the daily amount of protein recommended for a healthy diet. The RDA for protein ranges from 45 to 59 g per day for boys and from 44 to 46 g per day for girls. This works out to be about 7 to 8 percent of the day's total calories. High-quality protein (i.e., sources that contain all the essential amino acids) can be obtained by consuming eggs, meat, poultry, fish or dairy. Protein choices from nonanimal foods, such as soy, legumes, nuts, mixed grains and vegetables, are also possible options.

It's a She Thang

Make no mistake about it: The relentless media representation of the ideal teen body (think Christina Aguilera) has been hazardous to the body image of many impressionable young women. Girls tend to be more likely than boys to consider themselves overweight and to be actively trying to lose pounds. Weight loss methods include excessive exercise, meal skipping, 24-hour fasts, diet pills and an overall consumption of fewer calories and less fat. Unfortunately, cigarette smoking has also been linked to dieting in adolescents.

Parents can help their teenage girls avoid some of these dangerous behaviors by providing healthy and appealing food choices in the home. Allowing maturing girls to make and then "own" their nutrition decisions will help girls cultivate independence and will diminish the need for self-expression through disordered eating behaviors. It is also imperative that parents—especially mothers—act as role models for their daughters by demonstrating positive body image and stifling their own complaints about "needing to lose a few pounds."

Because young women tend to decrease their milk intake during adolescence, they also need to be encouraged to seek out alternate calcium sources.

> The relentless media representation of the ideal teen body has been hazardous to the body image of many impressionable young [teens].

Actually, because bone mass development occurs so early in life, girls should up their daily intake of milk and milk products prior to starting puberty. Parents can ensure that this is viable by making yogurts, low-fat milk and cheese accessible on a daily basis. . . .

Helping the Overweight Teen

Overweight teens face many challenges as they struggle to fit in with their peers and grapple with food choices and self-image. Developing the willpower to overcome these challenges is hard when temptation lurks at every fast-food restaurant and the only solace you can find is watching MTV for hours on end.

Responding to the rising number of overweight and obese adolescents, researchers have been investigating teens' energy intake and activity levels. One recent study, which examined the daily dietary intake of teens from 1988 to 1994, found that total energy intake had changed little from the 1970s to the years covered in the survey. This finding suggests that low activity levels may be the greatest culprit in the increase in teen obesity and that upping these levels may be the best solution for promoting weight loss.

> Girls should up their daily intake of milk and milk products prior to starting puberty.

To assist the overweight teen, providing sound nutrition choices at home is the first line of action. "Dieting," per se, is hardly ever appropriate for long-term weight loss and behavioral changes. In fact, encouraging a rigid, restrictive food plan will probably only increase a teen's stress and inner turmoil. A far better approach is to focus on the positive! Help the teen create lasting eating habits, like starting the day with a proper breakfast. Studies have shown that 20 percent of teenagers eat only two meals a day and that overweight teens are more likely than their peers to skip breakfast entirely. Teens need to understand that breakfast provides the energy they require to start the day on the right foot and avoid midmorning fatigue. Foods like whole-wheat toast, ready-to-eat cereal, instant oatmeal, a granola bar or a breakfast drink take little time to prepare and can satisfy the energy needs of adolescents.

Another way to accentuate the positive is to emphasize exercise and physical activity and de-emphasize sedentary activities, such as playing video games. Staying active will help improve body image and contribute to the success of gradually attaining and maintaining a healthy weight range.

A Winning Recipe for Teen Athletes

Research has shown that few teen athletes understand the role nutrition plays in their athletic performance. Teens who play sports have nutritional and energy needs that often exceed the dietary requirements of their less active peers. To help parents and coaches appreciate the unique health concerns of adolescent athletes, the American Dietetic Association (ADA) has issued a statement on nutrition guidance for teens in organized sports. The ADA recommends that teen athletes eat a balanced diet that includes moderate amounts of all types of food. The statement also discourages restricting foods based solely on their caloric, fat or sugar content. Finally, the ADA suggests that growth and activity can be supported by eating a diet that includes complex carbohydrates and adequate amounts of protein and fat.

To meet and sustain the extra energy needs of teen athletes, adequate calorie and nutrient intake is essential. A daily food plan should consist of three healthy meals with at least two snacks. Parents and coaches should also discourage unrealistic weight loss or weight gain goals. Teen athletes need to under-stand that unhealthy weight loss strategies are counterproductive to effective sports performance and can actually lead to fatigue, nutrient inadequacies, dehydration, eating disorders and impaired growth. In fact, unhealthy prac-

> Overweight teens are more likely than their peers to skip breakfast.

tices, such as seasonal weight loss regimens, can stunt growth and affect skeletal development. By trying to attain too low a body weight, female athletes can experience menses irregularities or cessation (amenorrhea), whereas male athletes may fail to grow as tall as they would otherwise.

To keep nutrient stores at an optimal level during an athletic event, teens should avoid skipping meals and exercising "on empty." Coaches and parents should offer (and encourage teens to eat) healthy snacks before and after exercise; snacks should be high in carbohydrates and contain moderate amounts of protein and little fat. Approximately three to four hours prior to the event, teens should eat an easily transported snack, such as a granola bar; fruit or raw vegetables; a peanut butter or luncheon meat sandwich; or some whole-grain, ready-to-eat dry cereal. Within the hour following the event, teens should replenish their energy stores by consuming a well-balanced meal or at least a high-calorie, nutrient-dense snack containing carbs and protein. Coaches and parents can encourage this behavior at team events by providing a cooler of snacks that all team members can share.

Hydration is also extremely important for teens who play sports, because adolescents do not tolerate temperature extremes as well as their adult counterparts do. Water should be consumed before, during and after any athletic event. If the activity lasts longer than 60 minutes, a sports drink can help restore blood glucose levels and aid in fluid absorption. . . .

Feeding the Mind

Getting teens to understand and appreciate the role of nutrition will not be a picnic in the park. Parents, teachers, coaches and mentors need to offer the right blend of guidance and independence, educating teens while also allowing them to make their own decisions. Teaching by example and providing healthy food choices for teens at home provide the recipe for fostering good nutrition habits that will last a lifetime.

Feeling Good Makes You Look Good

Deb Levine

Many girls suffer from poor body image because they lack sufficient self-esteem. In the following article, Deb Levine offers tips on how to improve your body image by improving your self-esteem. She maintains that the only opinion of you that matters is your own; if you consider yourself attractive, then you are attractive. She suggests focusing on qualities that you like about yourself rather than those that you do not like. Levine is a relationship counselor, health and sex educator, and social worker.

A t times everything seems to depend on how you look, even if you have friends, romance, and you could even have just aced that chemistry midterm. But, if you don't feel attractive, you may be unhappy. How we perceive ourselves is often predicated on how others view us. Teenagers everywhere worry about their weight, height and how they look. So, remember you're not alone. The anxiety that is created when this occurs will have us starving and stressing ourselves in an attempt to live up to unfair and impossible standards. There is no one way to look good no matter how you slice it; we're all different. But, when it gets down to the wire, it's what's inside that counts. If you can manage to feel attractive to yourself, in spite of what some others may think, then you are. It's as simple as that. Here are some tips for feeling good about how you look, everyday, all the time:

> How we perceive ourselves is often predicated on how others view us.

1. *Start from within.*

If you don't feel attractive enough, you'll come across as lacking confidence. Instead of outward appearance, it may be your self-esteem that needs to be built upon. Instead of wondering if you're a geek, try to pinpoint what it is that makes

---

Checking Your Own Self-Esteem and Body Image

If you have a positive body image, you probably like the way you look and accept yourself the way you are. This is a healthy attitude that allows you to explore other aspects of growing up, such as increasing independence from your parents, enhanced intellectual and physical abilities, and an interest in dating.

When you believe in yourself, you're much less likely to let your own mistakes get you down. You are better able to recognize your errors, learn your lessons, and move on. The same goes for the way you treat others. Teens who feel good about themselves and have good self-esteem are less likely to use put-downs to hurt themselves or anyone else.

A positive, optimistic attitude can help you develop better self-esteem. For example, saying, "Hey, I'm human," instead of "Wow, I'm such a loser," when you've made a mistake. Or avoiding blaming others when things don't go as expected.

Knowing what makes you happy and how to meet your goals can make you feel capable, strong, and in control of your life. A positive attitude and a healthy lifestyle are a great combination for developing good self-esteem.

Kim Rutherford, *Kidshealth.org*, October 2001.

you feel that way about yourself. Is it how you truly feel about yourself, or is it an image that others have impressed upon you? Hmmm. Looks like you got some thinkin' to do, huh? Yes, those pink polka dot pants might become a fashion craze next year. You never know! But if you really like them, then they're hot, and that's that.

> If you think you have great legs, make them stand out.

2. *Focus on your favorite qualities you possess.*

Yeah, yeah, I know, everyday is a bad-hair day for you, and you don't exactly have buns of steel. But c'mon, you've got to really look. Regardless of what anyone else thinks, evaluate you for yourself. If you think you have great legs, make them stand out. Maybe it's your lips. Accentuate your best traits. (Be tasteful, OK?) It will make a difference in how you carry yourself and how other people perceive you.

3. *There is no such thing as one-size-fits-all.*

Clothing with that tag is straight-up lying. Look around you: some of us have large necks and hips, others don't. Some of us have small calves and waists, others don't. It's also important to remember that we come in different shapes and sizes. Be mindful of your clothing sizes and how your clothes fit you, so you can achieve your desired look.

4. *Find a comfortable weight for you, then eat properly and exercise regularly to maintain it.*

Despite what advertisers often imply, everyone is not genetically created to be extremely thin. Remember, they're trying to sell a product, not necessarily to help you look and feel your best. Those pictures of glamorous, "flawless" supermodels are often airbrushed and shot at angles to make them look even thinner-than-life. Everything in moderation. If you do that, then you don't have to deprive yourself of those delectable, sweet, fatty treats (donuts, hamburgers,

French fries, whatever they are to you).

In the end, the key to looking good is feeling good. Spend less time comparing yourself to supermodels and celebs, and spend more time learning about your own body and what makes you feel sexy. After all, beauty is in the eye of the beholder, and the only beholder that really counts is you, Right?

Organizations and Websites

The editors have compiled the following list of organizations concerned with the issues debated in this book. The descriptions are derived from materials provided by the organizations. All have publications or information available for interested readers. The list was compiled on the date of publication of the present volume; the information provided here may change. Be aware that many organizations take several weeks or longer to respond to inquiries, so allow as much time as possible.

American Academy of Child and Adolescent Psychiatry (AACAP)
3615 Wisconsin Ave. NW, Washington, DC 20016
(202) 966-7300 • fax: (202) 966-2891
website: www.aacap.org

AACAP is a nonprofit organization dedicated to providing parents and families with information regarding developmental, behavioral, and mental disorders that affect children and adolescents. The organization provides national public information through the distribution of the newsletter *Facts for Families* and the monthly *Journal of the American Academy of Child and Adolescent Psychiatry*.

American Anorexia/Bulimia Association, Inc. (AA/BA)
165 W. 46th St., Suite 1108, New York, NY 10036
(212) 575-6200

AA/BA is a nonprofit organization that works to prevent eating disorders by informing the public about their prevalence, early warning signs, and symptoms. AA/BA also provides information about effective treatments to sufferers and their families and friends.

American Psychiatric Association (APA)
1400 K St. NW, Washington, DC 20005
(202) 682-6000 • fax: (202) 682-6850
e-mail: apa@psych.org • website: www.psych.org

APA is an organization of psychiatrists dedicated to studying the nature, treatment, and prevention of mental disorders. It helps create mental health policies, distributes information about psychiatry, and promotes psychiatric research and education. APA publishes the monthly *American Journal of Psychiatry.*

American Psychological Association
750 First St. NE, Washington, DC 20002-4242
(202) 336-5500 • fax: (202) 336-5708
e-mail: public.affairs@apa.org • website: www.apa.org

This society of psychologists aims to "advance psychology as a science, as a profession, and as a means of promoting human welfare." It produces numerous publications, including the monthly journal *American Psychologist,* the monthly newspaper *APA Monitor,* and the quarterly *Journal of Abnormal Psychology.*

Anorexia Nervosa and Bulimia Association (ANAB)
767 Bayridge Dr., PO Box 20058, Kingston, ON K7P 1CO
Canada
website: www.ams.queensu.ca/anab

ANAB is a nonprofit organization made up of health professionals, volunteers, and past and present victims of eating disorders and their families and friends. The organization advocates and coordinates support for individuals affected directly or indirectly by eating disorders. As part of its effort to offer a broad range of current information, opinion, and/or advice concerning eating disorders, body image, and related issues, ANAB produces the quarterly newsletter *Reflections.*

Anorexia Nervosa and Related Eating Disorders, Inc. (ANRED)

PO Box 5102, Eugene, OR 97405
(503) 344-1144
website: www.anred.com

ANRED is a nonprofit organization that provides information about anorexia nervosa, bulimia nervosa, binge eating disorder, compulsive exercising, and other lesser-known food and weight disorders, including details about recovery and prevention. ANRED offers workshops, individual and professional training, as well as local community education. It also produces a monthly newsletter.

Harvard Eating Disorders Center (HEDC)

356 Boylston St., Boston, MA 02118
(888) 236-1188

HEDC is a national nonprofit organization dedicated to research and education. It works to expand knowledge about eating disorders and their detection, treatment, and prevention and promotes the healthy development of women, children, and everyone at risk. A primary goal for the organization is lobbying for health policy initiatives on behalf of individuals with eating disorders.

National Association of Anorexia Nervosa and Associated Disorders (ANAD)

PO Box 7, Highland Park, IL 60035

(847) 831-3438 • hot line: (847) 831-3438 • fax: (847) 433-4632

e-mail: anad20@aol.com

website: www.anad.org

ANAD offers hot-line counseling, operates an international network of support groups for people with eating disorders and their families, and provides referrals to health care professionals who treat eating disorders. It produces a quarterly newsletter and information packets and organizes national conferences and local programs. All ANAD services are provided free of charge.

National Eating Disorder Information Centre (NEDIC)

CW 1–211, 200 Elizabeth St., Toronto, ON M5G 2C4 Canada

(416) 340-4156 • fax: (416) 340-4736

e-mail: mbeck@torhosp.toronto.on.ca

website: www.nedic.on.ca

NEDIC provides information and resources on eating disorders and weight preoccupation, and it focuses on the sociocultural factors that influence female health-related behaviors. NEDIC promotes healthy lifestyles and encourages individuals to make informed choices based on accurate information. It publishes a newsletter and a guide for families and friends of eating-disorder sufferers and sponsors Eating Disorders Awareness Week in Canada.

National Eating Disorders Association (NEDA)

603 Stewart St., Suite 803, Seattle, WA 98101

(206) 382-3587

e-mail: info@nationaleatingdisorders.org

website: www.nationaleatingdisorders.org

NEDA is dedicated to promoting the awareness and prevention of eating disorders by encouraging positive self-esteem and size acceptance. It provides free and low-cost educational information on eating disorders and their prevention. NEDA also provides educational outreach programs and training for schools and universities and sponsors the Puppet Project for Schools and the annual National Eating Disorders Awareness Week. NEDA publishes a prevention curriculum for grades four through six as well as public prevention and awareness information packets, videos, guides, and other materials.

Society for Adolescent Medicine (SAM)
1916 NW Copper Oaks Circle, Blue Springs, MO 64015
(816) 224-8010
website: www.adolescenthealth.org

SAM is a multidisciplinary organization of professionals committed to improving the physical and psychosocial health and well-being of all adolescents. It helps plan and coordinate national and international professional education programs on adolescent health. Its publications include the monthly *Journal of Adolescent Health* and the quarterly *SAM Newsletter.*

Websites

Dear Lucie
www.lucie.com

Lucie Walters writes a syndicated newspaper and online advice column for teens called Adolessons. Her columns discuss eating disorders, dieting, health, body image, and other teen issues. Visitors to the site can read archives of her columns as well as participate in message boards and chat rooms.

Teen Advice.Net
www.teenadvice.studentcenter.org

Teen Advice.Net offers students and teens expert and peer advice about health, body image, relationships, sexuality, gender issues, and other teen concerns. The webpage was created by The Student Center, a web community for college students, high school students, and teenagers.

Teen Advice Online (TAO)
www.teenadviceonline.org

TAO's teen counselors from around the world offer advice for teens on health, fitness, dieting, body image, family, school, substance abuse, dating, sex and sexuality, gender issues, and relationships. Teens can submit questions to the counselors or read about similar problems in the archives.

WholeFamily
www.wholefamily.com

This source is designed for both parents and teens. The site's advice columnist, Liz, answers questions about body image, dieting, fitness, teen sex, drugs, drinking, and pregnancy, while online articles discuss other issues such as divorce, relationships, and health.

Bibliography

Books

Arnold Anderson   *Making Weight: Healing Men's Con-flicts with Food, Weight, and Shape*. San Diego, CA: Gurze, 2000.

Frances Berg   *Afraid to Eat*. Hettinger, ND: Healthy Weight, 1997.

Brangien Davis   *What's Real, What's Ideal: Overcoming a Negative Body Image*. New York: Rosen, 1998.

Ophira Edut   *Adios Barbie*. Seattle, WA: Seal, 1998.

Ophira Edut   *Body Outlaws: Young Women Write About Body Image and Identity*. Seattle, WA: Seal, 2000.

Eve Eliot   *Insatiable—The Compelling Story of Four Teens, Food, and Its Power*. Deerfield Beach, FL: Life Issues, 2001.

Sandra Friedman   *Nurturing Girl Power*. Vancouver: Salal, 2000.

Debra L. Gimlin   *Body Work: Beauty and Self-Image in American Culture*. Berkeley: University of California Press, 2002.

Lori Gottlieb

Stick Figure: A Diary of My Former Self. New York: Simon and Schuster, 2000.

Cynthia Stamper Graff et al.

Body Pride: An Action Plan for Teens: Seeking Self-Esteem and Building Better Bodies. Glendale, CA: Griffin, 1997.

Heather Gray and Samantha Phillips

Real Girl, Real World: Tools for Finding Your Real Self. Seattle, WA: Seal, 1998.

Deborah Hautzig

Second Star to the Right. New York: Puffin, 1999.

Marya Hornbacher

Wasted: A Memoir of Anorexia and Bulimia. New York: HarperCollins, 1998.

Marcia Germaine Hutchinson

200 Ways to Love the Body You Have. Santa Cruz, CA: Crossing, 1999.

Mimi Nichter

Fat Talk: What Girls and Their Parents Say About Dieting. Cambridge, MA: Harvard University Press, 2000.

Harrison G. Pope

The Adonis Complex: The Secret Crisis of Male Body Obsession. New York: Free Press, 2000.

Richard L. Sartore

Body Shaping: Trends, Fashions, and Rebellions. New York: Nova Science, 1998.

Mary White Stewart

Silicone Spills. New York: Praeger, 1998.

Marilyn Wann	*Fat! So?* Berkeley, CA: Ten Speed, 1998.
Jonathan Watson	*Male Bodies: Health, Culture, and Identity.* Philadelphia: Open University Press, 2000.
Beth Wilkinson	*Coping with the Dangers of Tattooing, Body Piercing, and Branding.* St. Paul, MN: Hazelden Information Education, 1999.

Periodicals

Janice Arenofsky	"Teens Who Turned Bad Habits into Good Health," *Current Health 2*, May 1997.
Cindy Crosscope-Happel et al.	"Male Anorexia Nervosa: A New Focus," *Journal of Mental Health Counseling*, October 2000.
Robert C. Eklund and Theresa Bianco	"Social Physique Anxiety and Physical Activity Among Adolescents," *Reclaiming Children and Youth*, Fall 2000.
Dixie Farley	"On the Teen Scene: Eating Disorders Require Medical Attention," *FDA Consumer*, September 1997.
Carolyn Gard	"Think Before You Ink," *Current Health 2*, February 1999.
Beth Gooch	"Losing Friends, Losing Weight, Losing Control," *New York Times Upfront*, April 30, 2001.

Cynthia Guttman — "Advertising, My Mirror," *UNESCO Courier*, July 2001.

Christy Heitger-Casbon — "Back from the Brink," *American Fitness*, March 2000.

Betsy Israel — "Two Girls Talk About Food, Fat, Bodies, and 'Bones,'" *Redbook*, October 1997.

Phillipe Liotard — "The Body Jigsaw," *UNESCO Courier*, July 2001.

Susan McClelland — "Distorted Images, Western Cultures Are Exporting Their Dangerous Obsession with Thinness," *Maclean's*, August 14, 2000.

Celia Milne — "Pressures to Conform: The Thin, Shapely Look Can Be Dangerously Unrealistic," *Maclean's*, January 12, 1998.

Linda Mooney and Shelly Reese — "First, You Have to Accept Your Body," *Prevention*, August 1998.

Jennifer A. O'Dea and Suzanne Abraham — "Improving the Body Image and Eating Attitudes of Adolescents," *Nutrition Research Newsletter*, August 2000.

Diane Peters — "Don't Hate Me Because I'm Thin," *Chatelaine*, June 2000.

Cynthia Sanz — "Happy as They Are," *People Weekly*, September 29, 1997.

Ellen A. Schur,
Mary Sanders, and
Hans Steiner

"Dieting and Body Dissatisfaction in Young Children," *Nutrition Research Newsletter*, January 2000.

Stephanie T. Snow

"Fostering Positive Body Image in Children and Youth," *Reclaiming Children and Youth*, Fall 2000.

Katie Street

"Caloric Confessions," *American Fitness*, January/February 1998.

Selene Yeager

"Lose 10, 20, 30 Pounds or More!" *Prevention*, April 1999.

Jill S. Zimmerman

"An Image to Heal," *Humanist*, January/February 1997.

Index

135